Alpha Defender

Terry Bolryder

DEDICATION

To all the readers who asked me about these characters! You are all
awesome! <3

CONTENTS

CHAPTER 1

For the first time in her life, Lacey Matthias Wolford the third, known to most shifters as simply Matt, was not going to be a good little wolf.

She hadn't complained when she'd been raised as a boy in order to hide the fact that her father, the leader of the tribunal and therefore of all werewolves, had had only daughters. She hadn't complained when she'd been sent for him to spy on alpha challenges and mate claimings and had to report back on what she'd seen. She hadn't complained as she'd seen her sisters happily mated, knowing such a life would never be for her, because she was destined to lead their kind one day.

She hadn't complained because she'd thought there was a plan for her. And knowing what it was, always knowing what the future held, had given her a kind of control that she had desperately needed over the years as she pushed everything real about her down and played the part her father needed her to play.

But now he'd decided that one of his son-in-laws was trustworthy enough to lead the wolves, and he planned to marry her off in a political marriage to hide her from view and let the son everyone knew about quietly disappear.

Well, she'd be damned if she let him.

He'd dictated her whole life, and he'd not dictate another moment.

She shoved supplies into the backpack she'd borrowed from her sister's room. She put in extra pairs of breast wraps, since she didn't know how long she'd need to keep posing as a boy to stay safe. She put in bras just in case she had to go that way to stay undercover.

In her heart, she'd tried to be the man her father had needed. She'd felt useful, grounded. Special.

But it didn't matter any longer.

That future was gone, and along with it went the frail sense of superiority she'd clung to as she'd watched other females live a life she'd never know.

And now she had a chance at a life like that, if she could just find a place to hide from her father and his power. And she knew just who could help her.

It had been three years since she'd seen Thornton Wilder. Three years since he'd bullied her during the massive alpha games that had been held at a mansion for an unclaimed alpha female. She'd gone as a male to make sure things went okay, and for the most part they had.

Aside from Thornton, also known as Thor, being a tremendous bully. Back then she'd looked down on him. He'd been everything she didn't want. Huge, brutish, rough, an alpha without parents who had no regard for rules.

And he was exactly what she needed now.

He'd help her because he owed her big time. For his brother's life. When his brother had been caught by the tribunal and charged with treason, Thor had come to her, begging. It had been odd to see the huge man on his knees before her, head lowered as he begged for his brother's life. Her father had been away on business. She had the key to the holding cell.

After Thor promised that Lock (his twin) wouldn't hurt anyone if freed, she'd had to let him go. She tried to be hard, like her father, but in reality, her heart was soft. Too soft. So Lock had been freed and Thor had looked at her with a look in those warm amber eyes that was unlike anything she'd seen before. And he'd promised if he could ever return the favor, that he would.

She hoped he hadn't forgotten.

She finished packing and peeked out the door of her bedroom for anyone watching. She pulled the hood of the dark sweatshirt she was wearing up over her shiny blonde hair and started down the hall. It was nighttime and no one should notice. Her father would never guess she was running.

She hadn't yelled, hadn't screamed, hadn't put up a tantrum like everyone might have expected. No, she was too smart for that. If she'd protested, they'd have locked her up. One thing she'd learned from growing up with the tribunal as family was that the best thing to do was pretend you were loyal to them up until the moment you turned.

She padded quietly down the stairs, looked both ways in the huge, marble-floored foyer, noted for the last time how the moonlight looked blue across the pretty tiles, and then crossed silently over the floor and out into the night, leaving the door open behind her.

***

Thornton Wilder, known to his friends as Thor, stretched and looked out the window at the tree line in the distance. An odd thrill of excitement moved through him, and he wasn't sure why. He thought about taking a run, but even though it was nearly midnight, the pack business he'd been working on wasn't even close to finished.

He'd taken over as alpha when he'd inherited his parent's fortune and finally been able to throw his uncle out of the pack.

When his parents had died, leaving him and his twin Lock orphans, his uncle had taken the chance to turn the pack against them. He was bitter that the pure alpha blood in their veins meant that they would grow up and take leadership of the pack from him. Unless he destroyed them, which he had tried to do.

Beatings. Isolation. Hunger. All the punishments that would feel worst for a young animal who should be part of a pack.

And Thor had closed off for a long time as a result. Holed up deep inside himself and tried not to let anyone touch him. Became mean and strong, the type who wouldn't let anyone mess with him. Lock, his twin, his salvation, had been the one to protect him. The one to never lose his smile, even when he came back to their shack with bruises, the punishment for stealing the food he brought for them.

11

Lock had always been the sensitive one. The one who couldn't stand to see his twin suffer, and as they grew, the strength in Thor made him want to become the truly protective one. Where Lock solved problems with his smile, Thor solved problems with his fist. He was fast, strong, a true alpha, and he wouldn't let them hurt the one person in his life who had done something for him.

Thor sighed and looked out at the forest, wondering where Lock was now. He hadn't seen him since he'd gone to the tribunal and groveled to that brat Matt to free his brother. Matt, as the youngest pup and only son of the head of the tribunal, was everything Thor hated. Privileged, born to wealth and protection, thinking himself superior to everyone around him. He'd made that plain in the short amount of time Thor had gotten to know him when they'd shared a mansion during a huge alpha challenge involving eight other males.

He didn't know why Matt got under his skin so easily, why he kept wanting to pick the tiny male up and shake him. Why he couldn't help teasing him.

He was pretty. Of course he would be. All of the tribunal leader's daughters were gorgeous. The type of female Thor would have been destined for if his parents hadn't been murdered and his pack hadn't fallen into disrepute after his uncle took over.

Things were recovering now. There was much more money, thanks to some savvy investments, and multiple pack members were running clean, honest businesses that brought in revenue. And Thor had slowly tried to lower the walls around him to be a fair and more approachable leader, though he still heard subordinates refer to him as 'Thorns' occasionally.

He couldn't help that his guard defaulted to being up. He'd learned too often that if you lowered it, people beat you. Hurt you.

He clenched his fist and set down the pen he'd been signing forms with so he didn't break it. It was a beautiful night. From the two-story lodge where he lived and performed administrative duties for the pack, he could see a beautiful, grassy valley stretching out into a thick forest at the foot of high mountains. His pack made up most of a small town nestled in a remote area, and didn't bother the humans who did have the guts to settle there, despite the rumors of wolves.

The few males he'd had trouble with had left, and the other males were happy to have a strong leader who had good resources thanks to the work of his relatives. He'd make sure what was left to him increased, and he'd leave it to the next generation. Once he found a suitable alpha female.

But that wouldn't be easy. The last one he'd known of that was available to claim had been the one in the alpha challenge three years ago. Misty. And the fact that ten full alphas had shown up to compete just proved how scarce alpha females really were. When they were born to a pack, they were usually affianced from a young age to keep a bloodline going, and they had their pick of males.

But Thor could wait. He'd make sure whomever it was strong and a full-blooded wolf so that they could have shifter offspring. And if not, he wasn't in any hurry to get mated. He had enough to do already.

So when a loud knock sounded on the front door on the story below him, he rubbed his head and let out a deep sigh. Whoever it was should know better than to bother him at this time of night, when he could be sleeping. He wasn't, but he could be, and they didn't know any better.

He pushed himself out of his chair with a groan and slid his arms into his bathrobe, tying the sash around him as he went. He was wearing pajama bottoms but he didn't think whoever was knocking would appreciate him coming to the door bare chested. Well, maybe some of the pack females wouldn't mind, but their males would.

He crossed the wood floor of his lodge and over the large rug in front of the door.

He swung the door open and looked at the figure standing in the moonlight. Thin, soaking wet. Small, at least compared to him.

He took a step forward, toward the figure, which was drenched by rain and trembling slightly in the cold wind. Thor reached for the hood and pulled it off to reveal the face of the person he'd already identified by scent and stature.

"Matt?" he asked, astonished.

Pale blue eyes with long lashes looked up at him with determination glowing in their depths. "Thor. That favor you spoke of? I need you to return it."

Thor took a step back, allowing Matt to come into the lodge. Matt looked behind him briefly and then shut the door and leaned against it, letting out a huge sigh of relief in that high, feminine voice he tended to have. Even when he tried to sound gruff, it just didn't sound quite right.

"I'm safe," Matt said, sinking against the door.

Thor pulled his robe tighter around him and tried to figure out why exactly this man of all people would be here, now, in the middle of the night. And also, why the sight of him bothered him in ways that didn't

14

make any sense.

Matt stretched with a loud yawn and then slumped over to the nearest couch and curled up in it. Thor watched curiously, wondering at how small the thin man could be when curled up. With the hood back, Matt's blond hair shone softly around his face. His features were truly beautiful, as beautiful or more beautiful than his sisters when Thor had seen them. A thin, slightly upturned nose, pale, flushed skin, long lashes over his cheeks.

Thor felt blood rush to areas of his body it had no business rushing to and turned away from Matt with a hand over his mouth.

What to do? He knew he owed Matt big time, had promised to repay the debt he owed him for saving the one person who meant more to him than anything in the world. But he'd forgotten how confusing it could be to be around Matt. How it made Thor feel things he'd never felt. Made the mean part of him defensive, made the other part of him feel…protective?

He rubbed a hand over his face with a groan. It made no sense for him to be feeling all alpha over another male. Some males did prefer males, but he never had. Just this one, obnoxious troublemaker of a kid that seemed to get under his skin like no one else could.

He heard soft breathing and realized the kid had fallen asleep. He took a step toward him and looked down to make sure.

Yup.

He felt an urge to touch the other wolf's hair, to grab a towel and dry the drops on his cheeks. But he didn't. He just stood there, wondering if he should wake him and demand an explanation or just let him sleep and hope answers would be forthcoming when he woke up. He settled in a chair that faced the window.

Matt had said he was safe now and Thor would make sure that was the case. Whatever weird thing was going on between them, he had a debt, and he would repay it.

No matter how much his urge to put his hands on the other wolf made his eye twitch.

CHAPTER 2

Matt woke to see amber eyes the color of rich brandy staring at her warily.

It wasn't an emotion she was used to seeing from Thor Wilder. The man practically lived in overconfident-alpha mode, and she'd only seen him drop that facade once in her life, and that was when he'd begged for his brother's life.

She didn't know why he was so eager to save his brother. Lock had kidnapped Misty and almost handed her over to a criminal syndicate. It didn't matter that he had changed his mind, or that the criminals had been threatening Thor. In her mind, Lock had dug his own grave.

Except, she hadn't felt he deserved to die for it. And the tribunal had gotten oddly harsh in dealing with alpha males. Perhaps something to do with the dearth of alpha females and the intense competitions to win them? Would she face that now, if she revealed herself as an alpha female, or would the tribunal find her first, and silence her?

She shuddered at the thought.

"Penny for your thoughts?" Thor asked quietly, perching on the edge of his couch. Through his somewhat open robe she could see an intimidating, naturally bronzed chest with muscles only seen on Greek statues. He was impressively tall at a few inches over six feet, much higher than her own height of 5'9" which was tall by human standards for females. His hair completed his exotic coloring. It was a deep, rich red, almost a blackened brown, the color of black cherries in the shade. It was cut in a short, severe style that revealed the sides of his head and his forehead and stood in tousled tufts at the top. Utterly masculine. Perfect for putting her hands into it...

She froze, realizing that she needed to re-dose on the artificial male pheromones she was using. Otherwise, he'd scent her arousal at his body, his presence. She excused herself quietly, grabbed her bag and bolted for the nearest room with a door, shutting it behind her. She pulled out the vial and quickly dabbed it liberally on.

When she was satisfied that all traces of her alpha female pheromones were masked, she went back out to face Thor.

He was still studying her with that quiet, thoughtful expression. So unlike the Thor she'd known. That Thor was brusque, harsh, and more likely to start a fight or put his foot in his mouth than to get pensive or broody about something.

"You're different," she said, keeping her voice low and neutral as she sat back on the couch she'd slept on. The cabin around her was sparsely but nicely furnished, with carved wood furniture and generous cushions in a pine green color. A wide, woven rug sprawled over the wood floors, and a painting of a lake hung over the hearth, where a large fireplace stood encased in stone.

"How so?" he asked.

"Just... Quieter," she said.

"And you aren't," he retorted with a snort. "Just as obnoxious as always. Showing up in the middle of the night? It's not like I needed to sleep."

She yawned. "You owe me."

He folded his arms and she averted her eyes from the bulging muscles in his forearms and biceps. "I get the feeling you're going to keep reminding me. So why me?" he asked. "I mean, I know I owe you a favor, but you're with the tribunal. Get them to help you. Surely you know they have infinitely more power than me."

She hesitated, resisting the urge to bite her lip at the nerves that rose in her at his words. Of course they did. This wasn't a great plan, she had to admit that, but it was the only one she had. She hadn't exactly made a lot of friends as a spy for the tribunal, so the only option she had for help was someone who owed her.

"Don't look all worried about it. Of course I'll help you. Not only do I owe you, but I'm not afraid of the tribunal." He raised up to his full, impressive height. "I'm not afraid of anyone, actually."

Now that was the Thor she remembered. "Hm."

"I'm just trying to figure how what we're dealing with. I have a pack here, a small one, but we're doing well. If I seem different, maybe it's just that I have people depending on me now, and I have to focus on that more than just fighting the whole damn world."

That sounded oddly mature. Perhaps there was a whole side to him that she'd never seen.

But could she tell him everything?

"So what are you looking for now?" Thor asked. "A new pack? A new start? I can't imagine living here would be great after the way you've become accustomed to having things. Actually, I can't think why you've left at all. Maybe you should start with that."

He waited, and she gritted her teeth as she realized she really hadn't thought about how she would explain this at all. She'd only thought to run and she'd been drawn straight to him. Maybe not only because he owed her. Maybe also because of attraction.

She gulped. She was Matt Wolford the Third. She was intimidated by no one. Except she wasn't Matt anymore. She was Lacey now, and instead of being groomed to lead the race, she was on the run from a forced political marriage. Her eyes narrowed at the thought. At the gall that they could that to her after all she'd done, all she'd sacrificed.

"You look like you're ready to kill someone."

She just gave him a cold smile. He was right on the money.

"I don't hold with violence," Thor said. She was about to rebut that ridiculous statement when he amended it. "Not unless I'm the one doing it." One corner of his mouth quirked in a lopsided grin. "Okay, maybe I haven't changed that much after all. I'm just saying, you're in my pack territory, and I'm alpha here, and I won't allow you to commit transgressions against our laws without coming to me."

"I'm alpha as well," she grated out, trying to keep her voice low, which was difficult when she got emotional. She didn't want to submit to him. She wasn't ready to be a passive subordinate. She needed the protection of this place, but she didn't need him to order her around or prevent her from doing what she needed to. "I won't submit to you."

He raised an eyebrow and walked forward, arms folded, until he stood towering over her in front of her couch. "Oh you won't, hm?" He leaned forward and placed an arm on either side of her, caging her back against the cushions. She could feel his warm breath, the scent of woods and coffee, and something masculine and heady that made it hard to breathe. "And what makes you think not submitting is an option?"

"I'm an alpha. One of the tribunal—"

"But not anymore, are you?" he asked, tilting his head knowingly. "I think they've turned on you, so I think using them as a reason why you should out-alpha me is a rather stupid thing to do."

She bit her lip and avoided his gaze. "Then you should at least understand that this is a difficult thing for me to adjust to, and that I'm not ready to act in a way so different from what I've experienced."

He sighed and stepped away, putting one large hand up to his face. "I really don't need a spoiled brat running around here flouting my authority. If you want to challenge me for alpha status…" He ran his eyes doubtfully over her much smaller frame. "Go ahead and do so. Otherwise, you'll live by my rules as any of my subordinates in my pack would."

She took a deep breath, trying to calm the emotions whirling inside her.

She hadn't expected him to try and dominate her. She'd known he was alpha, and learned later on that his bloodline was actually very pure. But she hadn't expected to submit to him. It was trading one master for another. And if she knew one thing about people who tried to control you, it was that once they didn't need you, they'd throw you away. No matter how much they pretended to value you.

She sat there frowning as he paced to the kitchen. He brought back a cup and knelt in front of her.

"They really messed you up, didn't they?" he asked. When she didn't take the coffee from him he set it on a nearby table and reached to take her chin and force her gaze down to him.

She was humiliated by the tears she felt glistening in her eyes.

His expression hardened. "What did they do?"

She turned away, yanking her chin from his grasp so she could stare out the window at the wide-open spaces. The lush grass, the trees. She wished she could just run out in the woods and hide there. But she'd be found. She'd be unprotected. Not that Thor could do that much more, but he was an alpha, and a male, and he had certain rights while on his territory.

So she knew it was unreasonable not to agree to his demands. But something within her was just so tired of following the rules of a society that had utterly let her down. That had told her not to be a woman and then relegated her to that role with no notice, wanting to sell her off like an object.

In her opinion, losing control of a situation was unacceptable. It let people hurt you.

"Tell me," he said, trying to turn her back to him. She tried to resist, but his gentle strength was much, much greater than hers. "Tell me and I'll deal with them."

She shook her head. "You can't. Just let me hide here. I just need to hide until they stop looking."

"Will they stop looking?"

She gave him a flat stare. "Well, they wanted me to disappear, so my guess is that as long as I keep my head down, they may decide I'm not worth the effort. Or they may hunt me until my last breath."

"What do they want?" he asked in a low voice, holding her gaze with those hypnotic, honey-colored irises. His lashes were black and long, shading his eyes as he studied her. She resisted the impulse to squirm out from under that gaze.

Instead, she lifted her chin and tried to remember the regal bearing she'd put on for most of her life. When she'd been special, above others.

"They want something they can't have," she said.

"Do they want you to mate?" he asked, surprising her with his astuteness. "Seems odd, since there aren't many alpha females around. But if they had one, why wouldn't you want to mate?"

She didn't know how to respond to that. She tried not to let her puzzlement at how to answer show on her face.

"Ah, I see," he said. "You like males?" He nodded, as if deciding for himself that that made sense without caring if she actually confirmed it. "You know, that makes sense. I mean, Fifi is your cousin, and he likes it both ways, and then of course there are your pheromones."

"What about my pheromones?" she asked, curious what he meant.

He waved a hand. "Nothing. It's just… Never mind." He ran a hand through his hair, leaving it even more deliciously tousled. Damn, he was a fine looking male. If only she had been the type who could have considered…

But no, it was best to stay hidden. She'd stay the same boy she'd always been. And if Thor thought she was simply gay, all the better. Plus, it wasn't exactly a lie…

"Fine," she said, looking away as if embarrassed. "You're right, I do like males." And she did, but not for the reasons he thought. Was a lie of omission still a lie?

His face tightened in triumph. "I thought so. So what, they wanted to mate you to a female and you didn't want that, but the tribunal leader's son would never be allowed to be with another male, since they can't reproduce?"

"I'm sure it would be a hit to his image," Matt grumbled resentfully. "But yes, they want me to mate with someone I don't want to mate with, for reasons I can't abide."

"Abide." Thor grinned. "Fancy."

She snarled slightly at being mocked but relaxed when he went back to his couch and slumped into it with a sigh.

"So what do you need from me then?" he asked. "Protection, if they come sniffing? I don't really have a right to keep them away, you know. If we were mated, that'd be one thing, but well…" He shrugged.

Wait, that was true. If they were mated…

She eyed the huge man in front of her. Would it be so bad? It would be the ultimate 'eff you' to her family, and would ensure that they couldn't take her back.

But then again, that would just be letting them determine her future in another way. It still wouldn't be anything like having her own freedom.

"But no, I need an alpha female. I need to reproduce. Sorry, I can't. We'll have to think of something else."

"Right," she said, trying not to be disappointed. After all, mating wasn't exactly something she'd considered until recently.

He rested his head against his hands and thought for a moment. "I guess we could put you in a disguise? Dye your hair, something like that, so that if someone asked around, they wouldn't find you?"

She winced, because she already was in disguise.

He looked at her curiously. "Have you ever tried cross-dressing? I mean, what if we hid you as a female? They'd never find you then."

She swallowed, eyes widening. He was a little too close to the truth for her liking.

He stood, snapping his fingers like he'd had a light bulb moment and was extremely proud of himself. "That's it. We'll disguise you as one of the village females. Then you can live up here."

She hesitated. If she went along with this, would he really not realize she was a girl? He could be a bit slow about certain things. "I guess I can do that." She didn't really have a choice.

"I don't know what to do about your smell though," he said.

"If I shower, it should be less. I also probably have some perfume from one of my sisters in my bag." When he gave her an odd look, she explained. "I stole it in my rush to leave."

He sunk his fist into his other hand, satisfied. "See? Perfect." He helped her up and ushered her into the bedroom where she'd changed before. "This is the guest room, you can stay here. There's a shower through there. Get changed and showered, see if you can get some of that perfume on, and I'll get breakfast ready. When you're done, we'll see if you can pass muster." He laughed as he kept his hand on the bedroom door. "You know, I always kind of wondered what you'd look like as a girl. Probably hot, like your sisters."

She growled at him but he just winked and shut the door.

She sighed and pulled her shirt over her head. She put it on the bed in front of her and started to unwrap her chest bandages, when the door creaked open. She had only a second to react, and she shrieked and covered her chest with her hands, just as Thor came through the door, a shocked look on his face.

He averted his eyes, but then thought better of it, and turned back to her, aghast.

Oh no, he saw.

"This can't be happening," he said, scrubbing a hand over his face.

"You shouldn't have come in!" she snapped, pulling her shirt up to cover herself and lifting her chin imperiously. This wouldn't have happened if he hadn't opened a door she shouldn't have.

"You shouldn't be a girl!" he shouted back, flushing in embarrassment and finally turning away with folded arms. "If you had been a man, there wouldn't have been anything wrong with me opening the door to ask a question."

"I deserve privacy as a male, too!" she retorted.

He snarled. "That's a matter of opinion. So what the hell are you doing in my house, hiding the fact that you're an alpha female on the run from the tribunal? Do you even understand the trouble you've gotten me into?" He let out a sigh. "Oh my gosh, you're his daughter. I have the tribunal leader's daughter in my lodge. In one of my bedrooms!" He paced. "Fuck!"

She let out a slow breath. He had every right to be angry. He had every right to kick her out. She waited for his decision. It was his right to make.

CHAPTER 3

Thor didn't know what to do. She was beautiful. More than beautiful, she was gorgeous. And right now she was looking at him with defiant, vulnerable blue eyes the color of water under sunlight.

Waiting for him to make a decision.

He'd said he wasn't afraid of the tribunal, and that was true. But things got messy in his world when it came to alpha females. There just weren't many of them, and there was fierce competition for those that existed. And this one was the daughter of the leader of their whole race.

Dammit. What should he do?

His head flashed through his memories of her, berating himself for not realizing sooner that she was female. He'd picked her up, touched her, teased her, and tackled her in a football game.

He pulled at his hair with his hand, enjoying the delicious tension and the way the slight pain seemed to distract and calm him.

Why did she smell like a male if she was a female? He sniffed the air again. Yes, definitely male, but with an underlying note that made the hairs on his body stand up and take attention. He didn't understand. He took a couple stumbling steps back and slumped in a chair facing the bed. She still held her bandages around her, and he averted his eyes so she could change.

He wasn't a monster.

Just extremely confused. It all made sense, in a weird way, and yet he'd never considered that the tribunal leader's girly-looking daughter could actually be a girl. Alpha females were so valuable, why would the tribunal leader hide one?

Matt answered that question once she had her shirt on. "He wanted a son." She rested on the edge of the bed, head bowed slightly in defeat. It wasn't the obnoxious, headstrong, bratty Matt he was used to and he honestly preferred that Matt to this one.

"Is Matt your real name?" Thor asked.

She looked up at him with those piercing blue eyes. So very clear, like water from a mountain spring. "Yes. Unfortunately. My father wanted a son very badly. He worried that any son-in-laws would challenge him, and never wanted any leader who wasn't simply a figurehead so that our family could stay in control. His father had sons, and his father before him. We've always led the tribunal. So when my mother nearly died giving birth to me, and the doctor said there would be no more births, it was decided that I would take the place of a son."

"So what happened?" Thor asked, still trying to wrap his mind around the whole thing. "Why aren't you still in line to lead the tribunal? Seems like a sweet gig."

Matt gave him a bitter look. "It's not a sweet gig. I've had to hide who I was from the day I was born. I'm not even sure who I am anymore. But no, I'm not in line now. He's decided that one of my brother-in-laws is suitably docile to be groomed into the position and why have a fake male when you can have a real one? Plus, there was always the issue of how I would reproduce his genetic material if I was impersonating a male."

"True," Thor said. "Did he really think this through?"

"He covered his bases," she said. "If his son-in-laws hadn't thought he had a son, who knows if they would have been such suck-ups? But my sisters seem happy, so I can't really complain. As alpha females they had their choice of mates, and like my father, they tend to prefer pure blood."

"I recall you preferring it as well. What was it you called us? Mongrels?"

She shook her head. "I have a role. Playing it keeps me safe. And yes, I was told from birth I was superior to everyone around me. It was the only thing I had to comfort me. But give me credit in that, like you, I seem to have grown up somewhat in the past three years."

"Fine," he said.

"What used to be black and white is now all very gray and dark. I don't know what I'm doing or where I'm going. I just knew that you would help me."

He frowned. "Wait, so if a brother is taking over, what did they intend to do with you? Hide you?"

"Marry me off to a foreign dignitary. Keep me out of the public eye so no one knew his little secret. If anyone asked, which I doubt, tell them I abdicated and went to do peace work. I don't know. Let's be honest, it's not like everyone saw me as anything but that spoiled tribunal brat. I wasn't the intimidating alpha son he wanted."

Thor rubbed his chin. "Your family is all super feminine."

She let out a low growl. "Anyone who underestimates us is in for a nasty surprise though. Feminine or not, I've been taught to take care of business and I can." She eyed him disdainfully, sitting up a little taller. "So if you're getting any ideas now that you know I'm a female, I'd suggest you put them out of your head."

He grinned. Now that she mentioned it, he could definitely get some ideas. That long, slim body under his hands. He preferred curves on a female but soft and pretty and delicate looked good too. More importantly, she was an alpha female. And it just happened to be someone that had always intrigued him. And there was no one else here to challenge him for her. He could claim her and no one could do anything about it.

It might end in a challenge with the tribunal, however. But if he had to, he had packs he could call on for back up.

Either way, she was here now, and totally claimable. He was an incredibly strong alpha. His alpha abilities were nearly unbeatable.

But Matt didn't need to know that yet. What if she was a spy? Could he really trust her? Well, he had a hand up in that she hadn't meant to disclose her secret. If she tried to double-cross him, he always had that on her.

"What are you thinking?" she asked. "I can't tell what's going on behind that dark expression you're wearing and it makes me nervous."

"Well, first I was thinking that if I wanted to claim you, I damn well would and no one would stop me. Except for you, because I'd never force a female. Then I was thinking that it was possible you could be double-crossing me, but because I know your secret, I have more power over you than you could possibly have over me."

Her eyes widened slightly. "Oh."

"I was also thinking that I've wanted to claim an alpha female for some time, to build back the pack my parents were building when they were murdered. And here an alpha female is right in front of me, needing protection that I could offer best if I was her mate."

"Why you arrogant…" She stood, pulling on her hoodie. "I thought you'd be different, being so distant from them, but I guess an arrogant asshole of a mongrel is just as bad as an arrogant asshole of a—"

He cut her off with a hand in front of the doorframe, stopping her from leaving. Rage radiated off him as he placed a hand gently on her shoulder and pressed her back toward the bed. He caught her chin in his other hand and forced her to look up at him.

"I am not a mongrel," he grated out, leveling his gaze on hers to show her just who was in control. "If you insult my parents again, you'll be out of here faster than you can say your sorry."

She frowned but kept that imperious gaze in her crystal blue eyes. Anger flashed there. She was helpless to him but she was angry about it, and damn if it didn't turn him on that she had any response to him at all.

She was a proud, strong female, and it only strengthened his resolve to have her for a mate.

"I'll be damned if I stay here now. Not even one more second with you, mongrel—"

He pulled her chin forward and sealed his lips over hers in a firm kiss, stifling her weak struggle and wrapping a hand around her waist to pull her small body tight up against his. She pushed on his chest, and he nearly let go, but then she sighed and relaxed into the hold. Giving up, it seemed.

He slipped his tongue between her parted lips and explored the sweet depths within, loving the feel of her soft body against his. This was right, this was good, this was…

Pain erupted through him as she brought her knee up between his legs. He pulled them together quickly enough to block most of the blow, but it was still jarring. He put both hands on her shoulders and pushed her away from him.

She was flushed, red and extremely mad, angrily wiping his kiss from her lips. "How dare you? I've had some impertinent wolves in my day, males who didn't care if I was male or female as long as I was beautiful, but none dared take the liberty you just—"

With a light shove to her shoulder, he sent her sprawling onto the soft bed behind her. She let out an angry gasp and started to get up but he put out a finger and pressed it against her breastbone, stopping her with a startled squeak. She scooted back against the headboard and he stood back at the foot of the bed with his arms folded.

His groin ached slightly but if he'd had anything less than incredible reflexes, he'd have been unmanned. How dare she? She was enjoying that kiss and she knew it.

"Liberties?" he scoffed. "Taking? I'd say you were giving, princess."

She let out another offended hiss. "Giving? That's why I was struggling?"

"I thought you said you could take care of yourself," he said sardonically. "I thought you could handle any male who underestimated you." He smirked. "I guess not."

She took a deep breath, pursing her lips angrily as she adjusted her clothing from being pressed up against him. "You caught me off guard." She gestured to him, his height, whatever she meant by that. "There's just… a lot going on. And, well, most people wouldn't dare."

He remembered her earlier words and his gut twisted angrily in response. "But some have?"

She flushed slightly and looked away. "I took care of them."

He came around the side of the bed and sat on it. He reached up to touch her hair. It was short, just brushing the tops of her ears and curling down to her collar. So soft, so silky. It caught the early morning light and shone like champagne. "If you mated me, I would take care of all of them. I'd protect you with my life."

She gave him a glare. "And who would protect me from you?"

"You wouldn't want to be protected from me," he said, leaning forward to press a gentle kiss beneath her ear. The soft little lobe teased him and he caught it in his mouth. She let out a little gasp as he sucked it gently and then released it with a little nip.

"Don't do that," she said. But she didn't move out of the way. "I can't think."

He pressed her back down against the bed. "Then don't. Sometimes the best things happen when you aren't thinking."

She seemed to buy into that, leaning back to give him access to her slender neck so he could place kisses along it. He could take it more slowly with her, if that's what she'd wanted. But he could have sworn he felt her heat when he'd dragged her up against him and taken her mouth in a dominant kiss.

Most alpha females liked a dominant male. Especially now that males didn't fight as often for their favors physically, it was a way to display strength and ability as a protector.

And Thor knew she couldn't do better than him in that area.

She bit her lip and let out a troubled breath. "I can't. We shouldn't."

He kissed her lips again, deeply, and she groaned and opened for him. When he pulled back, she was looking at him with such star-crossed innocence that he realized a possibility he hadn't before.

"Was that your first kiss?" he asked.

She flushed deeply. "No."

It made him angry. He didn't know why, it just did. "Oh."

"But the rest…" She gestured to her neck, her ear. "That's new. I'm not sure how I feel about it." She sat forward and he instinctively reached for her to hold her against him.

It was a kind of tenderness that was totally new to him, but rose naturally in response to the overwhelmed feelings radiating from her. He wanted to keep everything away from her. Wanted to keep her safe until she relaxed and could focus on nothing else but him making love to her.

He hadn't realized how much desire for her was being held back by her former disguise. Now that he was seeing through that, it was nearly impossible to be the logical wolf he knew he needed to be for his pack.

He wasn't afraid to take on the tribunal. But his pack was still recovering and rebuilding after the wreckage his uncle had caused. And Matt would put all of that at risk.

He could feel her trembling in his arms. He tried to pull back to look down at her but she growled and stayed glued to his chest.

His eyes widened in wonder. If someone had told him he'd be holding Matt right now, after kissing her, he'd have fainted from shock. Instead, it felt so right. Well, except for the part where she was crying.

"Hey, it's okay," he said, stroking her back. She was so thin. He wondered if they could fatten her up a little now that she was here. She'd probably had to stay thin as part of hiding as a male. Male shifters rarely had any fat on them. Alpha females, however, were often lush and curvy.

"It's not okay," she said. "What we just did, that felt wonderful. I mean, yes, I hated it at first because I didn't choose it, but once you were gentle, I couldn't be distracted by fighting you, and it felt amazing." Her voice broke, but she pressed on. "And I'm just so damn angry that that's what he's been keeping from me all these years. I just feel so damn robbed and lost, and I feel powerless to do anything about it. How do you take that stuff back?"

Anger surged at him but he pushed it away because she needed him. It no longer mattered that she'd called him names. That had just given him the impetus to do what he'd been wanting to do for a long time. Take her in his arms and kiss her senseless.

But right now, he just wanted to give comfort. He cupped her face in both hands, surprised that he could want to be so gentle, and brought her in for another soft kiss. He pulled back, leaving her staring at him in confusion, her lips slightly parted.

"That," he said, wiping a tear off her cheek, "is how you take it back."

She blinked and then came forward to take his lips roughly in an awkward kiss. She was inexperienced, that much was obvious. Her tongue battled for entrance to his mouth in an aggressive way he'd never experienced from a female.

Nothing about it felt smooth or practiced. But somehow, it still felt freaking great.

CHAPTER 4

She kissed him roughly, surprised at the need in her own body, at how much feeling she had pent up inside her that seemed to be exploding out all at once the more she touched his incredible body.

So long she'd wanted males, so long they had been off limits. The secret had been more important, her father's wishes, her father's plans.

Now he could go screw himself, and she could screw Thor, if she wanted to.

Though she'd tried to be a man for a very long time, she was becoming aware that there was actually a very hungry woman underneath.

She growled and used all of her strength to flip their positions on the bed. His surprise made him easy to move, and she shoved his shoulders hard and rolled on top of him to pin him down. Not that her weight could do much, but judging by the shocked arousal on his face, he wasn't going to object.

Damn, she loved this feeling. Her small hips settled over his powerful abdomen. She could feel the ridges of his six-pack, feel the wolf in her taking over, the powerful alpha female who had always wanted to be free. She nuzzled at his neck and then reached for his waistband.

He let out a muffled grunt and put a hand out to stop her, but she flicked it aside and he sighed.

"Wait, Matt."

"Lacey," she said. "Matt is my middle name. My first name is Lacey."

"Lacey," he said, putting a hand up to touch her hair. "That's a perfect name."

She flicked her gaze up at him, irritated that things were slowing down. "Why?"

"I don't know," he said. "Maybe because there's something delicate about you."

"I'll show you delicate," she growled, struggling against his hand to pull down his pajama pants.

He let out a frustrated breath and caught both of her wrists in his easily. She growled and tried to pull away but the grip was like iron. "Hold on, don't do something you'll regret," he said.

"I won't regret this. Who knows when they'll come for me? I want to live for right now. I don't know what will happen in any moment after. For once, I just want to live."

He hesitated, holding her and looking her over as he made his decision. She prayed inwardly that he didn't resist her. A wall inside her had broken and she needed whatever was behind it to flow out. And she needed to do it with him.

"You said you'd show me how to take it back," she said, slowing her breathing to try and sound calm and reasoned. "You kissed me."

He blinked. Those warm amber eyes could be so mysterious sometimes. "I did."

"Do more," she said, struggling to get her hands free so she could put them on him again. "Let me do more."

He grinned, finally making his choice. He shook his head and used her trapped hands to pull her off him and then rolled so that she was beneath him and he was on top. "I'm afraid I very much like to be the one doing. So if you want what I have to offer, sit back and relax."

She snorted. "So cheesy. So you're going to go all alpha on me after all? So—" She gasped as a loud tearing sound interrupted her mocking of him. She looked down to see the soft jersey pants she'd been wearing shredded in two and tossed to the side. She was bared to him in her panties, and curled up slightly in shock. He moved a hand to her hips, keeping her beneath him, under his control. The air in the room moved over the exposed flesh of her legs and she bit her lip as his hand ran over the soft skin.

"My pants," she said.

"You need new ones anyway. We'll need to get new everything." He reached for her shirt and lifted it over her head, then leaned forward and pulled down the edge of the loosened bandages with his teeth, lightly grazing the flesh beneath. She'd never been touched there and she flushed and arched against the foreign sensation.

"You smell amazing," he said. "Like wildflowers, but bitter, and cold. Let me warm you."

She sighed as he gently pressed the coverings aside and lightly covered each breast with his hands, kneading the flesh gently and bringing blood back into them where they'd been trapped. She looked down to see the marks of her bindings. She was so used to them, but seeing the rage in his eyes as he tilted his head and stared at them, she realized how bad they really were.

"Your father is a monster," he said. He cupped her gently and rubbed a thumb over the top of one nipple, making her gasp. "This must have hurt, every single time you did it. Every day of your life. Not to mention the danger he put you in. Unprotected."

He continued to softly torture her breasts with both hands, bringing them to life. She writhed slightly, unable to believe this was happening to her.

"I don't need to be protected," she replied breathlessly.

"You do now," he said. "I'm never letting you go back there."

"You barely know me," she said. "All we've done is fight."

"You helped me," he said, laving her nipple with his mouth. The warm, slightly rough texture made her buck up off the mattress and he caught her with one hand on her back but kept his mouth on her breast, gently sucking and swirling his tongue around the point that was becoming an agonized center of desire.

"I had to," she said. "I couldn't—"

"Shh," he said. "Just focus on me, what I'm doing to you." He slid a hand between her legs. "Making you wet. Making you want me."

His low voice was hypnotic. Was this really the man she'd argued with? Had that just been her way of avoiding the attraction she'd never be able to act on? It was confusing, but right now her body and her wolf ruled the situation. Her wolf had been trapped too long, and now she was running full speed through the forest, toward freedom, and she wouldn't be stopped.

"Mmm. You feel amazing," he said, sliding a hand underneath to touch her intimately. She bit her lip as a flash of pleasure moved through her, heating her and making her shake with his touch. He rubbed over the place just above her center that was aching for release, pressed slightly down on it, and she squeaked in surprise. She tried to squirm away from the sensation, but she was glad when he used a strong hand to stop her, to keep her grounded. He hooked a hand under the waistband as if to pull off her underwear and she put her hands up to her face, embarrassed.

He paused, and she lowered her hands to look at him.

"Is something wrong?" he asked. "I don't want to do anything you don't want."

"No," she grated out. "It's just confusing. And slightly embarrassing. I mean, so much attention to a part of me that wasn't supposed to exist."

"Oh, it was supposed to exist," he said, leaning down to place a soft kiss just above the top of her panties. "It was supposed to exist for me."

She loved the feel of his rough breath, those hard lips. If only he'd move a little lower.

No, that was too intimate, too soon. She squirmed against the lust raging inside her, begging her to come to life and take everything he could give. To take him inside her, unsheathed.

The thought was a mad one, but she didn't care, not as long as the euphoria surging through her didn't stop.

He planted his hands on either side of her head and looked down at her. "I can take it slow."

"I don't know if I can," she said.

"You're so innocent," he said, pushing hair off her forehead, where it was dampened with sweat. Her heartbeat thrummed rapidly because he was close. "I don't want to take advantage."

"I'm inexperienced, but that doesn't mean I'm innocent. I know I want your cock, deep inside me, taking me hard, right now."

"But you flush when I want to bare you naked."

She felt herself flushing deeper. "Don't mock me."

"I'm not. I just want this to be good for you. Not tainted by embarrassment."

"Then make it good," she said mockingly. "You're an alpha male, aren't you?"

His face tightened and he nodded. The heat was still there in his eyes, but it was colder. "It takes two to tango."

43

She gritted her teeth, pressing her legs together at the ache that wouldn't seem to go away. "If you don't want me…"

"Oh hell no," he said, cupping her breasts in his hands and bringing them together as he stroked. Fire surged again inside her. "I want you right now. Right here. But I want all of you, and I want you to be able to say you were ready."

"I'm ready," she said.

"To be mated?" he asked.

She tried to sit up at that. "No."

"I thought not. So rules?" he asked.

"Anything but that," she said. "You should know how to avoid it." Unprotected intercourse would mate them, anything else was safe.

His expression darkened slightly. "I do. But do I want to?"

She bit her lip, and his eyes caught the movement and followed it hungrily. She could feel his want for her. Feel the animals between them engaged in a dance for dominance, a curious parry of wills to see if they were a match.

She wasn't sure. Was he?

"Don't make this so serious," she said. "Just give me what I want."

"So, you want me to know what you want better than you do?"

She blinked. That was actually a perfect description of what she wanted. "Yes."

"Fine," he said, lowering his mouth to place a wicked kiss on each of her nipples. "I'll do my best."

CHAPTER 5

He kissed up to her neck, experimenting to find the places she liked best. She curled deliciously at nearly every spot he touched. Her body was pliant and responsive in his hands, like she was made for him, waiting for him. She made the wolf in him howl, made the man in him feel like he was about to come home.

She looked up at him with those bratty eyes and told him exactly what she wanted, while telling him nothing at all. She was a total mystery, but she was *his* mystery. His alone. And now that she was here, he was never going to let her go. His wolf surged under his skin, wanting to take control. Wanting to dominate and overpower, but he forced himself to take it slow.

He kissed the back side of her neck as she turned to the side and she let out an electric gasp. His eyes widened and he ran a hand down her side, grazing her spine. She writhed, looking at him with wide eyes, and he grinned. He flipped her over so that she was facing away from him, underneath him on the bed, her smooth, gorgeous back and neck in front of him.

He lowered his head to kiss up her spine and she lifted her ass in the air in invitation. He grinned and leaned over her, putting a hand between her legs to feel her as he kissed that spot on the back of her neck that made her gasp and moan with ecstasy. Ecstasy that was heightened as his hand found a rhythm between her legs, stroking her soft, wet velvet in time with her little moans as he kissed her neck, bit lightly along the back of her shoulders, laved with his tongue all along her sensitive back.

She thrust back to meet him, her body moving in time with his as she lay under him, and his hand dipped into her warmth, just one finger, then another, testing, stretching, listening to the sounds she made, the beautiful scent in the air. He was fully in control of the situation and he loved it. He was throbbing and hard but he didn't care. All he cared about was the rising pleasure in her body, the movements becoming more frantic with the rising heat. He could feel her muscles starting to tense and relax as he kissed her back and rubbed in circles with his fingers over the wet nub where her pleasure was centered.

She called his name, she called for mercy, and she bit down against the onslaught of pleasure that he was bringing her to, but none of it made any difference. He knew the moment the release hit her by the frozen position of her body, and then the long, low scream as she arched against him, pulsing against his hand and calling his name. It was the most beautiful thing he'd ever seen, smelled or felt.

She was his.

Or she would be. But for this kind of ecstasy he could be patient. As long as no one else ever touched her. He could feel how overwhelmed she was, the shock at what she'd been missing. Damn, he could kill her father for what they had done to her.

He let her relax slightly beneath him, listening to her murmurs of amazement. Then he started again, rocking his hips as he moved his hand against her, stroking, teasing, letting her feel him as she adjusted to the sensation. He was rock hard, and wanted badly to be able to come inside her, so he was glad he had pants on and could resist. He wanted this to be about her. Wanted her to see just how much he could do for her body. What a good mate he would be.

He wanted to win her, simply by showing her pleasure. And then he wanted to pleasure her for the rest of his life.

It was so odd but so right, and he was done fighting it. So was she. She dug her hands into the sheets and arched up as his fingers explored. He circled her with one finger and then plunged it deep inside and she mewled.

"That's it sweetheart, and when I'm inside you, you'll feel a thousand times better."

She simply growled slightly at that, probably because he had stopped moving, and so he gave her what she wanted and resumed stroking gently with his finger inside her. He removed it from her wetness and swirled around her clit again.

"How does it feel?"

She whimpered in response and he grinned.

"Good."

He let his body come more in contact with her, enjoying the feel of his bare chest where his robe had come open against her soft back. He kept his hand wrapped around in front of her to reach her and keep pleasing her, and let himself imagine that their bodies were one at this moment.

She cried out and threw her head back and he caught her in a rough kiss from the side, stifling her cries as she came, giving her an anchor in an uncertain universe.

They weren't Matt and Thor anymore, they were just two wolves, two humans, lost in something cosmic and amazing and incomprehensible. And it was amazing.

He kissed her until her screams turned to gentle whimpers as she relaxed down in front of him. He nipped at her ear and she gasped, rearing back sensitively. He wanted to go further but could hear from her labored breath that she was exhausted. He turned her over, desperate to look into her eyes.

They were so blue, glowing from the pleasure he'd given her. Gratitude shone in her eyes, and he felt triumphant. Alpha. He planted his hands on both sides of her head and kissed her again. Roughly. Harshly. Letting her know who was master. She simply wrapped her hands around his neck and let him know she was just as much his master as he was hers.

He growled, liking it.

And then a knock sounded on the door. He raised his head and she froze, the moment broken. Both of them held their breath. The last thing he wanted was someone coming in right at that moment, with the scent of her heady in the air. He'd likely have an alpha challenge on his hands.

He put a gentle hand on her shoulder to reassure her, and then quietly got off the bed, wrapping his robe tight against him as he went. He peeked out of the room to look at the door. With his advanced hearing and scent, he knew who it was. His Beta, Ernie.

Well, that was good because he had needed to get in touch with him anyway about the situation. Not that he planned to tell him everything, but he would need him to go pick some supplies up for him.

He looked over at Matt, Lacey, who was rolling languidly in the covers to pull the sheets over herself. She was flushed, glowing, beautiful. And yes, a little pissed off.

So his little she-wolf had wanted more pleasure? The thought pleased him. He rubbed his chin and looked back at the front door.

"I'll be right back," he said. He would need to go to the kitchen to get his phone, which was on the counter.

"Don't leave me," she said. "Don't let him in." She looked with wide eyes in the direction of the door. "He'll—"

"Scent you," he said. "I know. And I damn well don't want anyone else near you right now."

She nodded hesitantly.

"Trust me," he said.

"Okay," she said warily. He loved the way her cheeks were flushed with color, the way her eyes were almost too blue.

"I'll be right back," he said. He waited for her to nod and then went out to get his phone. He'd get rid of Ernie without letting him inside, and then he'd be back to talk with his she-wolf.

They had things to discuss.

***

So that was sex, she thought in amazement as she leaned back against the soft, comfy pillows with the slightly rough covers. No high thread-count Egyptian cotton here. But she thought that there were other things here to make up for it. She blushed deeply, and that's when he walked back into the room, sliding his phone into the pocket of his robe.

It was still deliciously open, showing a wide expanse of chiseled chest, and she licked her lips. Alpha males were something to behold.

"Like what you see?" he asked.

She nodded. "Well enough."

"Good," he said, walking forward. "Because I'd like to mate you."

Silence fell over the room. She felt her heart thump in her chest as shock moved through her.

"What?" she asked.

"Mate you," he said. "You're alpha, I'm alpha. We're obviously compatible. You come alive under my hands. Yes, I've decided you'll do."

Pride rose up in her in an unwelcome wave. "Excuse me?" She sat up, pulling the covers over her. "You've decided I'll do? Who said I wanted you, mongrel?"

He smirked. "Are we going to play that game, then?" He gave her body a long, appraising look, and she felt her treacherous blood heat up as he did it.

He was right. She wanted him. But mating? That was serious. He'd kissed her and she'd wanted to experience more of what he'd promised. But mating? That would be permanent, irrevocable. And could have lasting consequences for everyone involved. Far more than simply her and Thor, but also his pack, her pack, and neighboring packs.

They barely knew each other. They'd spent more time fighting in the short moments they'd been together in the past, than they'd just spent wrapped in pleasure together on the bed.

"Why?" she asked. "Why now? You barely know me."

He shrugged. "I'm a wolf. I know when to follow my instincts."

"What about my instincts?" she said. "What if I still want to sow wild oats? I've only just started living."

He growled and a dark, possessive expression moved over his face like storm clouds over water. "Sow wild oats? I don't think so."

She shook her head. "It's not your choice."

"What do you want from me?" he asked. "You've only been here a day and you're already driving me crazy with mixed messages."

"My life is a mixed message. I'm powerful, I'm not. I'm valuable, I'm worthless. I need to let everyone see me, and then I need to disappear. And I'm not going to cow to you now, no matter how good you make me feel, because this is the first time in my life I'm making my own decisions and

I'm not going to hand that over to anyone until I'm good and ready."

She scrambled off the bed, grabbing her shirt and putting it on as she went. She rummaged in her backpack for another pair of pajama pants and pulled them on.

Thor watched.

When she felt covered, protected, she sat back on the chair by the bed, willing her body to calm down, for the heat he'd created in her to subside. She felt itchy under her skin. Every instinct in her urged her back toward the bed. But she'd been ignoring her instincts for a long time.

"What is it?" he asked, keenly attuned to any show of distress from her.

She rubbed her hands over her face and exhaled roughly. "Everything. Gosh, things changed overnight. And I came here expecting begrudging protection. Not for you to discover I was a female and possibly want to mate me. We used to fight…"

"I know. Maybe it was because our wolves knew something we didn't, and it stirred us up inside. I don't know. But as to me possibly wanting to mate you, there's no *possibly* about it, sweetheart." He stood and walked over to her chair. He sat on the edge of the bed, facing her with folded arms. "I want you. Now. And why shouldn't we? We're both alphas. We'd have strong young. I think you're more than attracted to me. It's kind of a funny story, if you think about it. Perfect to tell cubs."

"Hmph." She bit her lip.

"Give me one reason why we shouldn't. It would ensure my pack line, protect you from your family, and feel damn good. I think we'd even grow to love each other."

She bit back a sardonic grin. *That* she wasn't so sure of. But she didn't need that in a relationship. Hot sex would be fine. Commitment and freedom would be fine. Having her own life would be fine. But with Thor, would she have her own life, or would she just be living under his power, subject to his whims?

She realized now that she was a powerful prize, one any alpha wolf in the area would try to win if they knew she was female. Perhaps Thor was just taking advantage of her obvious attraction to take a prize he wouldn't have had otherwise.

She didn't even know much about his pack.

"How did your parents die?" she asked.

His expression tightened, his bronzed skin went slightly paler and he turned away from her with a dark look on his face. He ran a hand through his short hair and looked out the window. When he looked back at her, he was the cold Thor she'd known before.

"Ah, so that's what it is?" he asked, folding his arms tight. "Worried I'm too mongrel for you?"

She sucked in her cheeks. That hadn't been where she was going at all, but she had a feeling that now that she'd pushed this particular button, there was no going back even if she did try to explain. "That's not—"

"Got it," he said, interrupting her. She couldn't blame him for being upset, not after what they'd just shared. But she also couldn't just go along with whatever he wanted. "So I'm good enough to pleasure you, but not good enough to be your mate?" He waved a hand as he stood. "Got it. *So* got it. Fine. Shower. Clean up. Make sure you aren't a liability, because others may be visiting soon. Pack members."

"Am I going as a boy or as a girl?" she asked.

He frowned. "A boy. Clearly, you do crazy things to male minds as a girl. I don't need a daily alpha challenge just because you're here."

She tightened her lips into a frown but nodded. "Fine."

He narrowed his eyes, looking her over. "We can talk about options for keeping you disguised when we've both had a chance to regroup." He shook his head with an exasperated sigh. "Heaven knows I need it."

"Fine," she said.

He shrugged and closed the door behind him, and she let out a long breath of relief.

She'd hurt his feelings, that was for sure, and she hadn't meant to. But she couldn't just go on taking any plan any male got it into his mind to suggest. She needed to think clearly, which she couldn't after multiple orgasms from a super hot male.

She hadn't yet even thought of who she would want to mate. She needed time to feel safe, to adjust, to see just how far her father and the tribunal would go to reclaim her.

In the meantime, she would just have to resist Thor and his sexy wiles. No matter how hard that was.

She threw a towel over her shoulder and strode into the bathroom to take that shower he'd suggested. The rest could wait.

CHAPTER 6

Thor paced in his bedroom. The cold shower he'd taken hadn't done anything to calm the anger or ardor racing in his veins.

She'd asked about his parents. His parents! As if she had any room to speak, as the daughter of a complete psychopath.

It was true in the world of wolves that survival of the fittest meant that more respect tended to be given to families with more surviving members, but his parents hadn't just died due to illness.

They'd been murdered. In cold blood. By someone they trusted, according to Lock. Someone they hadn't expected. They hadn't been weak, unless you called trusting others weak. No, whoever had ambushed and stabbed them in the back, literally, was the weak one.

Them, or whoever had arranged it. He cracked his knuckles and paced more frantically, his long strides eating up the floor space in the small bedroom.

The shower noises from the direction of her room stopped. Thank goodness. Now he could stop picturing what she looked like naked.

Maybe.

He tried to remind himself of pack business he had to take care of. He needed to meet with Ted, who'd had a piece of equipment in his office break and couldn't ship things for his business.

Then he had to check in with a few families whose males were working abroad, make sure the females were happy and that no one was misbehaving. And that their needs were being met.

He'd have to try to avoid Lilac, a wolf he'd grown up with who had a long-time crush on him. She'd never been anything but a friend to him, but he just couldn't seem to communicate that to her no matter how much he tried.

And he needed to figure out how to hide Matt, Lacey, whoever she was, from anyone who tried to hurt her. She'd awoken the protector instinct in him, big time, and he couldn't turn it off just because of a few offensive words or an ugly question.

The longer he paced in his room, the more he knew what destiny must have been trying to tell him all along in his fascination with her. She was his fated mate.

Oh, who could have guessed that the brat he'd bullied and hated for being part of the tribunal was destined to end up in his bed as his mate? It was almost too much to imagine. Lock would laugh...

His heart clenched as he realized Lock might never know. Was he even okay? He hadn't taken the time to check in in so long, Thor was beginning to give up hope. It was especially humiliating after how he'd humbled himself on the ground in front of people he'd hated to save his life.

He'd gone to Fifi and Fifi had brought him to Matt, and he'd known as he looked into the little brat's eyes that he didn't want him to hold his brother's future in his hands.

But he'd been surprised by Matt's mercy. By the way he didn't even expect Thor to grovel, seemed almost horrified by it. He (she) had taken care of things with barely a word, certainly with no guilt leveled at Thor, and Thor had been surprised by his equanimity. He'd looked back at Matt as he left and wondered *just who is this person?*

Well, the question hadn't been answered because the question was wrong in its very principle.

It should have been, "*What* is this person?"

A quiet knock on the door sounded and he opened it to see Matt waiting there. Her chest was flat again, bound underneath a thin tee shirt that was under a zipped jacket. No one would question the layers here. It was cold in the spring, wet and rainy often times. If Matt wore jackets every day, no one would notice.

That is, if Thor even let him out of the house.

Matt blinked nervously, arms folded defensively over her chest. *Lacey,* he reminded himself. *I need to stop calling her Matt.* Except there was something affectionate about a girl called Matt. It was just so her.

He ran his tongue over his lips as he looked at the area where her breasts were bound beneath her shirt. How he longed free them, watch them spring forth into his hands, petal pink nipples begging for his touch. She reddened and looked up at him like she could read his thoughts.

"That's not going to happen again, in case you were wondering," she said. "At least not for a good while."

"Oh really?" he asked, leaning against the doorway with one arm. "Think so?"

She gulped and took a long look up and down his body. He laughed and she froze and gave him a cold glare, her eyes glacial. "Think so? I *know* so."

He chuckled and moved past her into the kitchen. He'd heard her stomach growl and knew she hadn't eaten. Brat or not, she should be fed. All females should be.

"Don't walk away when I'm talking to you," she grumbled, hands clenched.

He shrugged and started pulling pans out from under the counter. Then he paused and pulled his phone from his pocket. He swiped it open and checked for texts from Ernie. He should be here soon. Ernie was his second in command, his beta and his half cousin. He'd been born to his uncle and another female in the pack that he'd potentially forced.

Ernie's mom had escaped the pack and Ernie had been allowed to stay after Thor's uncle and cousins had been chased off, mostly because Ernie had been as wronged by Thor's uncle as Thor had.

All Thor wanted to do right now was cook breakfast for the sexy, aggravating alpha female in his kitchen. To keep showing her that them mating wouldn't be something controlling and rushed, but simply something *right*.

She stared at him expectantly as he pulled ingredients from the freezer. It was like she thought she could read his mind if she just glared long enough.

"Making scrambled eggs, is that okay with you?"

She shrugged one shoulder and pulled the magazine he'd had out on the counter toward her. "Hunting and Fishing?" she asked.

He felt his neck warm slightly. Sure, he hunted with his claws and fished with his teeth, but yes, he enjoyed the human magazine. Would she mock him, as she tended to mock anything human?

"I'd like to do some hunting while I'm here," she said. "We had mandatory wolf time back at the compound, but it wasn't like I just got to run free in places like this." She gestured to the beautiful lakes, streams and forests portrayed in the magazine.

He sniffed the air as he cracked eggs into the pan. She'd gone back to wearing her synthetic male hormones. Heaven knew she needed them. Her face was beyond pretty, and any male would be suspicious in an instant if it weren't for the fact that most of them weren't very aware of the scientific developments in artificial pheromones.

He hadn't been aware of it when he first met her, that was for sure.

He served eggs and cheese onto a plate and slid it toward her. She ate it absentmindedly while reading the magazine.

He sat next to her, watching each morsel as it moved into her perfect pink lips, unable to believe he could feel jealous of *eggs*. "There are some amazing streams and lakes around here. I'd be happy to take you out to look at some."

She nodded. "That would be satisfactory."

He shook his head and started to clean up the kitchen. She was so entitled and she didn't even know it. Well, she could figure that out later. Right now she just needed time to adjust.

A knock sounded on the door, and he wiped his hands on the dish towel he was holding and strode to the door. That would be Ernie, bringing the things he'd told him to bring for Matt. He cast a quick glance at the smaller wolf seated at his counter, and sincerely hoped Matt could fool Ernie if the need arose.

***

Matt watched with narrowed eyes as the young, gray-haired man greeted Thor and pulled him into a rough hug. Thor pulled back to look the other man in the eyes and asked him questions in a low tone that said he didn't want her to hear. She cocked an ear, then noticed the new man looking in her direction and quickly turned away, ears burning.

She didn't need excess attention and Thor should have known that. She thought over what the man at the door looked like. There was something vaguely familiar about him, but she couldn't make it out. The silver hair looked odd with his mid-twenties features, and he had a masculine face, square and plain with friendly but slightly empty blue eyes. Just medium, regular blue.

She felt a shiver up her spine. She didn't like the way he looked at her. She didn't even know why.

She'd been creeped on a lot in her work for the tribunal. The fact that she was a tribunal official hadn't stopped a lot of wolves, male and female, from thinking she was there to be dominated. Simply because she was small and pretty, at least for a male. Well, she'd show anyone who thought they could bother her.

She was strong and able to fight. She'd done it countless times, using her body to get out of trouble when she couldn't do it with her mouth alone.

She laughed darkly to herself. Next time Thor tried something she'd make sure to show him who was boss.

As long as her mutinous body didn't melt at his touch first.

He wanted to mate her. Her. Her body felt warm at the thought and she squirmed on the stool, trying not to think about it as she focused on the fish and game in the magazine Thor had on the counter. Fish and game weren't sexy.

An image of her and Thor splashing out of a stream as wolves, playing and biting, and then making their way to a soft patch of grass together, laying down in the…

She shook her head. *No way in hell!* She flipped frantically though the pages as the men continued to talk in low voices. She heard scuffing on the ground, and turned to see that the other man had pushed past Thor to come over to her. She turned on her stool to look at him imperiously.

He froze in place for a moment under her cold stare. She'd learned it from her father and more than a few men had fallen victim to it, unable to keep doing what they were doing when so much haughty disapproval was leveled on them.

It was an alpha stare, one of her powers.

The man glared at her for a moment and then looked back at Thor, who caught up to him and pulled him back roughly by the shoulder and turned him around to say something else in a low voice.

She slipped off the stool and walked over to them, not liking the secrecy or feeling like she had no control over the situation.

"Who is this?" she asked Thor, circling the newcomer as Thor held him.

"This is Ernie," Thor said. "My second in command."

She sneered, letting Ernie see it. "Your beta?" She looked him up and down. "Were there no others to challenge for it?"

Ernie scowled, but she refused to be cowed by it. Thor seemed to think she was being rude, but Thor didn't understand what she saw. That Ernie wasn't a good wolf, and that the only way to deal with him was by letting him know up front that you wouldn't take any crap from him.

She'd gotten to know far more wolves in her day than Thor ever would and she could read them well.

Ernie handed a bag he'd been carrying to Thor. "The things you asked me to get," he said in a low, gravelly voice. He smirked as he looked her up and down, making her skin crawl. "I can see why you need it. She's sure to stand out."

"You mean he," Thor said.

Ernie raised a dark gray eyebrow. "You're kidding. I assumed it was a girl in boy clothes."

"Can't you scent it?" Thor asked, sharing a quick glance with Matt to make sure she didn't say anything.

Ernie scented the air. "Ah, you're right." He laughed, and it was a sound she didn't like. "I guess the face just threw me off." He reached for her and she moved away, but he caught her around the waist and tried to turn her face to him. "So pretty, though."

Bile rose in her at his touch and she heard a low snarl from Thor. Things were about to get complicated.

CHAPTER 7

Thor growled and lunged forward to separate them, but before he could, he heard a loud crack as Matt's head ducked and her leg swung into the air in a fast spinning kick that whacked Ernie's hand away from her and put her a pace or two away from him. She grabbed the bag from Thor's hands and let out an angry hiss and strode away into her room.

"Call me if you need me," she said, before slamming the door behind her.

Thor rubbed a hand over his neck. "Damn."

Ernie groaned and held out his busted-looking hand. "I think she broke my damn wrist."

"Hmm," Thor said coldly. "You'd do well to stop thinking of *him* as a she."

Ernie nodded reluctantly. "Damn, it hurts."

"It'll heal quick," Thor said. "What were you thinking, grabbing him like that?"

"I still can't believe that's a him. In fact, I don't think I even care." He took a step toward the door Matt had exited through.

Thor stepped in front of him, growling. It was a much lower, more threatening sound than he'd used before, and Ernie stopped.

"Fine." He shook his head and folded his arms. "You're going to need more than a wig for that one. That kind of beauty isn't going to stay underground very easily. What's his name?"

Thor hesitated. He wasn't good at lying, at intrigue. He was an honest person and generally expected the same from others. But for some reason, he didn't really feel like sharing anything about Matt with Ernie. "He's a family friend," he said.

Ernie raised a brow. "Really? I didn't know your family had any friends."

Thor felt a lump in his throat. Had Ernie always been this much of a jackass, and he just hadn't noticed?

It hadn't been easy coming back to take over the pack, and he'd been glad to have a beta who was happy to assist. But he wasn't the most sensitive of males and so if Ernie had had some bad personality quirks, he wouldn't necessarily have noticed.

"Nevertheless, he's a friend, and I'll expect you to treat him with respect." When Ernie gave him an odd look, he cleared his throat. "As long as I'm alpha here."

Ernie nodded, but continued to look at Matt's door with a strange gleam in his eye. "Don't you want to claim him? I know it's odd, because he's a dude, but there's something…weird…about him."

Thor clenched his teeth at the other man's mention of wanting his mate. That's right, he was already thinking of her as his, try as he might to slow himself down. Her hot little body had told him everything he needed to know. Now he just needed to give her time to come to the same conclusion.

Time without someone like Ernie sniffing around.

"If that's all, then you can go. Thanks for picking things up for me," Thor said, ushering Eddie, who was still sneaking looks at Matt's door, out of the cabin.

"Fine." Eddie seemed reluctant to go, but Thor needed to go talk to Matt.

"Ernie, I need you to play this one close to the chest, okay? There are some big people involved."

Ernie nodded. He'd never given Thor a reason not to trust him, and if he'd sided with his Thor's treacherous uncle, he could have done irreparable damage. Luckily, he seemed to have as much reason to hate the man as Thor did. "All right. I understand."

"And if you put hands on him again…"

Ernie raised his hands. "I get it, I get it. Odd pheromones. I blame the pheromones."

Now that was the Ernie he knew. He shuffled him outside and shut the door behind him, locking it. He could hear angry cursing coming from the direction of Matt's room.

He walked over cautiously, listening to what she was saying. Something about "impudent males"…

The door banged open. "If you're going to eavesdrop, you might as well come in."

Thor's jaw dropped. Matt was standing at the door, hands on her hips, the short black wig he'd had Ernie buy atop her head, covering her blond hair. Her eyes looked even lighter by comparison, her eyelashes and eyebrows had nearly disappeared.

But there was no disguising her beauty. She took his breath away. Maybe she always had. Maybe it was destined somehow. Certainly no female had ever gotten under his skin as much as Matt did, even as a male.

"You look great," he said.

"Think it'll work?"

"I think if they find you, they find you. But in the meantime, at least if anyone is asking around about a missing blond wolf, they won't find them."

She nodded, turning to a mirror on the wall of her room to pull the short pieces of the wig into place. "It's itchy."

"I'm sure," he said. "Want me to take you out and show you around to distract you?"

She nodded. "Sure. Let me get my jacket." She shrugged into it and Thor led the way out of the cabin.

They walked down a dirt trail lined with gravel, enjoying the smell of the wet grass, the fresh mountain air. He was pleased to have her at his side. It already felt just right. He could see her living here with him. Having cubs here.

But would she be able to see the same thing? Would he ever be more than a mongrel to her? Would anything he could give her feel small compared to what she'd had before?

They walked until they came to a stream that led to a small pond. It was glistening in the morning sun, partially shaded by clouds and the mountain just behind it.

"It's beautiful," she said.

He was pleased. He couldn't give her the world and its millions. But he could give her a little stream, a little pond, and mountains to run wild in. Maybe at some point she'd stop missing the other stuff.

"I'm glad you think so."

She looked up at him with a happy smile and his heart thumped in his chest. No one had ever affected him this way.

Was it just that he knew she was a female now? No, it was something else. She was being honest and open, letting him see the person behind the mask.

Not to mention she'd melted like hot butter in his arms and made the wolf in him stand up and howl in pleasure.

She picked up a stone, studied it for smoothness, and then chucked it out across the lake, watching it skitter, making little ripples across the surface. "Wow. That's oddly satisfying."

"I know," he said, picking up a stone, studying it, and then sending it skimming out across the water, twice as far as hers. He grinned at her.

"Show-off," she teased. She started walking around the side of the pond, through the tall grass, and didn't seem to mind that her shoes and pants were getting wet. "Damn, I love the smell out here."

"It's nice, huh?" he asked. "After living here, I don't think I could ever be a city wolf."

There was a small beat of silence, as he realized the implications of his words. She knew he wanted to mate her, and he'd just said that he couldn't be in her world. How would she react?

"Me neither," she said.

His grin deepened. She was perfect. His groin ached at the thought of showing her again just how perfect she was.

He could hardly wait to mate her.

She walked a little further and then sat down on a log to rest and look out at the water.

"Tired?" he asked, sitting beside her. The log leaned perilously under his weight and he groaned and took a nearby boulder instead.

"Fatso," she said playfully.

"Hmph." He flexed his arms, enjoying the way her cheeks flushed as she checked out his muscles. "Really?"

"Whatever," she grumbled, looking away.

"And what about you?" he asked. "You're so skinny."

She shot him a glare. "Skinny or not, it's not polite to comment on women's bodies."

He shrugged. "I'm not a very polite person then, I guess."

"That, my friend, would be the understatement of the century."

He frowned. The word "friend" ricocheted through him. He should be glad they were friends instead of enemies. Instead, he just sort of felt vaguely unsatisfied, because friends wasn't even half of what he wanted. "So what are you going to do if they don't find you?" he asked. "Make a home here?"

"Or move on," she said. "Hide somewhere new. As long as I'm free, I don't mind."

"A life on the run, no one to depend on? That doesn't sound like my kind of freedom."

She gave him a meaningful look and then stared out at the lake. "You've never had my kind of prison."

"This is true," he said quietly, watching her. "I'm sorry. I'll respect what you want."

"It's like, just because I came here in a moment of crisis, that doesn't mean you should take advantage," she said. "What if I don't want to take a mate? What if it would be too weird after living as a male for so long?"

He shrugged. "I didn't think of that. All I thought about was the fact that you were just what I'd been looking for and it would help you, too. It would makes things less complicated."

"How does making a decision to be mated for life make things less complicated?" She shook her head. "Besides, you deserve to mate for other reasons."

"What reasons?" he asked.

"Love, like you mentioned. Not out of convenience."

"I need to mate with someone who will benefit the pack. I need an alpha female."

"And if you can't find one?" she asked.

He threw another rock out across the lake. "Then I guess I'll stay alone."

She exhaled and leaned back on the log. Over here by the edge of the pond, the smell was murkier, earthier, but still rich and moist and a delight to be next to.

If she wasn't here to stay, at least he could give her something nice while she was here. Though something in him just fell apart at the thought of her leaving.

"So, if you mated me, it would only be because you finally found the alpha female you were looking for?" she asked.

He couldn't read her expression, but he expected there was more to those words than just the spoken part. "Yes, but not only because of that. I'm attracted to you."

"What if you hadn't found out I was female?" she asked.

"I admit I was a little attracted to you either way. But the thing is, I need to procreate. I need to further my pack. I need someone who can stand beside me as we rebuild everything my parents have."

"And I could never do that, could I?" she asked. "Because the minute the tribunal heard, they could try to ruin you."

He blinked. Was she right? No, he'd ruin the tribunal first. "They can try," he said. She sat up a little straighter, looking over at him.

"Not much scares you, does it?" she asked.

He shrugged and tossed another rock. "I guess not. I mean, I grew up getting the crap beat out of me by the only parental figure I had. Me and Lock had no one. After you almost die, what is there to be afraid of?"

"It happening again?" she said, resting her chin in her hands.

"I'm not a kid anymore," he said. "I had to rely on those around me back then. But now I'd like to see anyone try and take away the man I've become."

She tilted her head. "With words like that, you might convince me to be your mate after all."

He grinned. Jackpot. "Well, maybe I've re-thought it? After all, as you said, you could cause me trouble."

She sniffed. "You should be so lucky."

He tossed a rock and laughed. "To be with a cross-dressing tribunal lackey?" He rested his hands on his knees and looked over. "Sure."

He frowned when he realized he'd hit a sore mark. Damn, why did one of them have to hurt the other's pride any time they were opening up?

Dammit!

She folded her arms. "I get it. I was horrible to you. To all of the others back at the mansion. And I have nothing to justify the superiority. Except it was all I had. I knew I would never have the life others would have. I wouldn't be able to have a mate—"

"You can have one now—"

She put up a hand. "I knew it would never be the same. That my future would be chosen for me, that no one around me would ever know who I truly was. I'm not saying that made it okay for me to be a bully. Just that there are usually reasons behind someone being hurtful."

"I know," he said. "But there are also people who are just plain jerks."

"Like you?" she asked. "You judged me from the first second you met me just for being the son of the tribunal leader, didn't you?" She stood next to him and threw a rock out. It was a good, hard throw, and her rock reached the same place his had. Impressive.

"I suppose I did. I had a real problem with authority for a lot of years. And then I finally get a chance at an alpha female at that mansion years ago and someone like you shows up."

"Except as you now see, I had zero interest in that alpha female."

He grinned. "Are you sure? Misty was hot, all curvaceous, and—"

She cleared her throat. "No. I'm sure. I'm sorry you prefer curvaceous though. Looks like the only alpha female available is a little lacking in that area." She looked down at her chest and then shrugged.

He nodded. "Nothing a little feeding couldn't fix." He gasped as he found himself pushed off balance, right into the cold water in front of him. He went in face first, coughing and spluttering, and felt for the bottom before pushing himself up. He came up treading water angrily, looking at the little miscreant who'd pushed him in.

It seemed she'd acted without thinking, because she was looking at him with a mixture of guilt and terror at what she'd done that he found particularly satisfying. At least he would, once he dragged her in with him. He came toward her menacingly. She tried to back up but he caught her hand.

"Oh no you don't."

She squeaked and struggled against his hand. "Wait, I'm sorry, I just…"

He grinned and yanked in her into the water with him, enjoying her screams as he dunked her in the icy depths. As she came up, cursing and stomping away from him, he shook his head and laughed.

At least life with her would never be boring.

She sent him a glare over her shoulder that said she'd make him pay for this when she was dry, and he gave her an answering look that said he was looking forward to it.

Then he followed her inside.

CHAPTER 8

He had lunch ready by the time she came out of her room, dried and dressed. She leaned on the counter with a sigh.

"That pond water was so cold," she said, shuddering.

"Well, not everyone has a private pool, princess."

She sat on the stool and watched him cut the sandwiches he'd made into careful halves. "I wouldn't have expected you to be so domestic."

"I've been taking care of myself a long time," he said, setting a plate in front of her.

She lifted the sandwich and bit into it, starving.

"So why did you push me in the lake?" he asked. "What's wrong with me saying I could feed you?"

She looked down and considered the sandwich but seemed to realize that there was no point turning down good food. And Thor knew he made some damn good food.

She sighed. "I guess it's just a hot button for me. Someone saying they can change me, or control me, or that I would work for their purposes if I was just a little different."

He felt like an ass, realizing how like her family he had sounded. "I'm sorry, I won't do it again."

She shrugged and kept eating, ignoring him. So she was still pissed.

"Look, it's like you said before. All you can do is try to be better." He sat next to her with his sandwich but let it sit as he thought of what he wanted to say to her. "But I can promise you this. As long as you're here with me, no one, not even me, is going to force you to do anything."

She looked up into his eyes and he caught his breath at the vulnerability he saw there. "Really?" she asked. "And how will you ensure that?"

He didn't answer. He didn't know how to. He just knew that his body would stand between her and anyone who meant to hurt her. It was just biology. His wolf said so.

She picked at a piece of lettuce that had fallen from her sandwich. "I don't even know what I expected when I came here. Maybe I was intrigued by you. Maybe I wanted to use the favor you owed me. All I know is that I didn't think it through, and I usually think everything in life through. Maybe this instinct thing you've been talking about is correct."

His heart thumped. Did she mean what he thought she meant?

"I'm willing to look into it, at least. Maybe."

"I appreciate that."

She shrugged again. She had a habit of it, and he was used to watching those thin shoulders go up and down. Used to seeing her bow her head in regret or indignation. Used to watching her negotiate the difference between what she actually wanted and the choices available to her.

It was a life he couldn't imagine.

There were people depending on him, but he had chosen for it to be that way.

They finished lunch quietly, both lost in their thoughts. When they were done, all Thor could think about was taking her back to his room and sealing the deal. But that wasn't an option, so he stood to start cleaning up.

"Get some rest," he said. "Just spend the day inside. Tomorrow, when you're at one hundred percent, you can come out on my rounds with the pack if you want to get out of the house. They'll like you, I think."

"Do they like you?" she joked.

He tilted his head to the side and considered it. "I don't know. But I'm working on it."

"That's all you can do," she said, standing and grabbing his magazine to take it to her room.

"Hey," he said.

She gave him a wicked grin that made his breath catch in his throat. He wanted to pounce on her. "I guess I'll see you tomorrow then, wolf." She let her hips sway slightly as she walked to her bedroom and shut the door.

Damn, that female was going to drive him nuts. He grabbed his notebook and went to his office to try to focus on work. Tomorrow things would probably get even more wild, and he was looking forward to it.

***

Her first day doing rounds with Thor had gone well. They'd spent time visiting anyone who needed something fixed, checking in on the sick, and trying to find out if anyone had heard rumors about a missing tribunal wolf. The pack had been welcoming, though that may have had to do with the fact that some of them were still really intimidated by Thor.

But even those wolves seemed to be won over by his care and loyalty.

She couldn't blame them. She was being won over as well. They walked out of town along a dirt road that led up into the woods and toward his cabin.

Thor stopped and took a long stretch in the sunlight. She wet her lips and tried to look away from the bulging muscles on the powerful alpha beside her.

"What do you think?" he asked, snapping her out of her thoughts.

"What?" she asked, stupefied by hormones.

"About the village?" he asked, a gleam in his eyes.

"Oh," she said, embarrassed by the trail of her thoughts. "It's wonderful. Beautiful scenery and location. Really nice people. They seem wary though. What was your uncle like?"

He paused. "My uncle?"

"You know. The one that was alpha before. The reason you have to rebuild."

"How did you know?" he asked.

"Didn't you mention it?" she asked. "Either that or just something I heard when they had Lock in custody."

His expression darkened and he continued up the path. Shadows from the woods grazed the dirt in front of them, and then threw spots over his shoulders as they walked further into the trees.

The trees were amazing. Large, rising, deep-green pines and pale, quaking aspens. Delicate plants and brush beneath, and rich mulchy soil. It was a wolf paradise and Matt never wanted to leave.

Things just felt simple here. Sure, there was still work to do with the pack, to keep things strong and make sure outsiders didn't come in and try to mess things up, but it was workable.

Unlike the mess that was *her* life.

"What are you thinking?" he asked. "You're quiet."

"You never answered about your uncle," she said. "What's going on there?"

He shrugged those massive shoulders and walked on. "Not much to say. He was abusive, happy to take over when my parents were gone, and never let me and Lock forget that we were a threat to him."

"That's too bad," she said. "It sucks to be betrayed by your own family."

He paused and sent her a meaningful gaze. His eyes were a deep warm brandy color in the shaded light of the woods. "You would know," he said.

She flushed, pain coursing through her like blood. "Yeah, I would."

He jogged a few feet ahead of her and then stopped, facing her with folded arms. "So what do you think? Could you live here?" he asked.

She swallowed. She'd be lying if she said she hadn't been wondering the same thing. Could she adjust to life somewhere like this, even if it was safe? Or was it just the fact that it was new and free? And then there was the tribunal to consider.

She opened her mouth to answer. "I—"

Thor looked over their shoulder at the sound of approaching footsteps. She shut her mouth, somewhat grateful for being saved from answering.

She turned to see a short, curvaceous she-wolf huffing her way up the path. She had dark brown hair tied back in a long ponytail, was in her mid-twenties, and had a diamond shaped face with curious gray eyes. She wore a black sports jacket with jeans and anger flashed in her eyes as she looked at Matt.

Then she passed her and ran straight to Thor, wrapping her arms around him.

Thor raised his eyes to the heavens as if asking for patience and then pulled her off of him.

"Lilac, for the last time…"

"Come on," she said. "Stop fighting it."

He sighed as she latched herself on again and Matt stifled a laugh and looked away.

"What are you laughing at, bitch?" Lilac asked.

That did it. Matt turned to her, glaring. "Excuse me?"

Lilac squinted at Matt and her expression lightened. "You're a boy?"

Matt nodded slowly, though a part of her wished she could reveal herself as a female and show this she-wolf just how she felt as an alpha female watching someone touching her alpha.

Wait. *Her* alpha? Ridiculous. So why did she want to challenge this insolent female for dominance?

"Lilac, I've told you…" He sighed and gave up, leaving the small female glued to his waist as he started to introduce Matt. "Anyway, I'd like you to meet Matt. He's a visiting alpha male…"

Lilac's interest perked immediately and she sized Matt up once again. Oh no. No no no. Matt looked at Thor for help but Thor seemed to have just realized that he could shove his problem off on her. A wicked gleam lit in his eye.

"Yes. He's here looking for a mate," he continued.

Matt's eyes widened and she promised Thor silently that he'd pay for this later.

"Does anyone else in the village know?" Lilac asked, biting down on her lower lip and showing one wolfish fang.

"No," Thor said. "Can you keep it a secret? We don't want him being mobbed."

Lila nodded, finally letting go of Thor so she could circle Matt. Unexpectedly, she tore out of her clothes and changed into a little brown wolf, trotting around Matt and scenting the air.

That was smart. Wolves had better senses in wolf form, and she wondered why no one had done it before. But she had faith in the pheromones.

Lilac sniffed a few more times and then seemed satisfied. "Okay. Do you guys want to go for a run? I was about to go out when I saw you." She grinned. "And you know I like to come over when I see you." This smile was reserved for Thor, and Matt didn't like it at all.

Well, Thor wasn't the only one who could manipulate the situation. Manipulation was her middle name. She frowned, because it wasn't flattering, but oh well.

"Lilac, was it?" Matt said. "I'd love to go run with you, but I have stuff to take care of back at the mansion. However, I hope next time you see us, you won't only come because of Thor."

Lilac's gaze snapped up to him and he could almost see little hearts circling her head. Matt made a beautiful boy and she knew it. Thor didn't stand a chance. And if attracting Lilac's attention to herself was the only way to keep her off of Thor, so be it.

She reached down to pet Lilac's muzzle and Lila snuggled in, as if submitting to an alpha. Matt sent a triumphant glare at Thor and realized he was glaring back darkly.

Lilac looked up and between them, and then took a step back. "Am I missing something?"

"No," Thor said. "I just better get back." He grabbed Matt by the arm and jerked him along with him as they left. "Get back home Lilac, your mom isn't feeling well again today."

"Shit, all right," Lilac said. She took one last, longing look at Matt and then picked up her clothes in her mouth and ran off in the direction of her house.

Matt watched her go in amusement. That had gone well. She'd successfully shifted the female's attention onto herself, thereby preventing competition for Thor.

She was about to turn to him with a triumphant grin when she was yanked against his chest and his mouth came down on hers. Hard.

CHAPTER 9

His hot lips seared hers as he crushed her to him. He forced her lips open and delved in with his strong tongue, stroking and exploring. Owning. It was suddenly hot, despite the cool mountain breeze swirling around them.

His hands dug into her waist, dragging her against him, thigh-to-thigh, stomach-to-stomach, a full possession of her from head to toe. Everywhere she grazed him felt on fire. Though she knew they weren't in the best location for this, she was too overwhelmed to do anything but submit to his will. It felt so good to be wanted so badly, like he couldn't breathe if he didn't have her.

He growled lightly and nipped her lower lip. She let out a little gasp as her knees went weak and an ache throbbed at the apex of her legs.

She heard a rustling in the woods and her survival instincts kicked in, reminding her that this wasn't the time or place for such things.

She pushed against his chest but he didn't notice. He was just so much stronger than her. So she harnessed all of her self control to draw back her leg and give him a swift kick in the shin.

He released her with a grunt, jerking back to rub the sore leg. "What was that for?"

"We're in public, you idiot," she gasped out, putting a hand over her heart as if it could calm the pounding within. "You'll blow my cover. You just told everyone I was a visiting alpha male, remember? So what would they think if you were kissing me?"

"That I was kissing another alpha male?" he asked. "It's not like it's unheard of for males to mate."

"Or maybe they'd catch on that I was a female. They're all one step from figuring it out anyway," she said. "I don't know why it's harder to hide this time."

"Maybe because I'm here, bringing all of your femininity to the surface?" he joked pompously.

She turned and growled, pointing a finger at him menacingly. "Don't even."

He laughed and put his hands behind his head and followed her up the road. "Okay. For now, princess."

She sent him her best glare and kept walking up the dirt path. Sunlight was streaming again as she got closer to the edge of the tree line.

His heavy footsteps thudded behind her and then his warm hand caught her elbow and turned her toward him. His eyes were intense, no longer playful. The same way he looked before he kissed her.

"Why were you flirting with a she-wolf? Is there something I should know about your preferences?"

She shook her head and yanked her arm back. "I thought it was obvious. I was just trying to get her off of you before I blew my cover by challenging her for dominance."

"What?" he asked. He took a step back, looking puzzled. He was always so masculine, so in-control, from his short dark hair to his hard, chiseled features. But right now, he just looked confused. Stunned. It was an interesting look for such a large alpha male.

"Don't look so surprised. I'm considering you as a mate after all. I expect better behavior than letting other females wrap themselves around you at any moment."

The astonishment in his eyes turned to pleasure and he followed her as she started for the cabin again. "Can I help it if females want to wrap themselves around me?"

She sighed. So egotistical. But not without reason. She looked him over. Well over six feet tall, heavily muscled, with that handsome, classic face and elegant squared-off jaw. And those burning brandy eyes that could make you drunker than any alcohol.

Yes, females definitely would throw themselves at him.

"Well, here is one female who can resist," she said snippily, hating the mental image of other wolves liking Thor.

"Oh really?"

"Really," she said tersely, speeding up her pace as she could hear him closing the distance.

"So you aren't even a little tempted?" he asked in a gruff voice.

"No," she lied, feeling her body betray her even as she said it.

"I can smell you, Princess," he said, catching up and wrapping an arm around her waist, caging her against him, making her his. She'd never belonged to anyone but herself, so it was an odd moment. But for some reason she just wanted to sink against him and feel safe.

He held her tightly with both arms and nestled his nose in her hair.

"You smell amazing. I know you want me."

"Stop that," she said, fighting the rising pheromones in the air. His scent was amazing. So spicy and warm. He nuzzled her neck and she felt aches in places that had no business aching. "Someone will see," she gasped out.

"Let them," he said. "No one can touch you when you're with me. I'll protect you from anything. Anyone."

"Thor…" she said.

"I know," he said, his big body encircling her. "I'm being unrealistic, aren't I? But I loved seeing you with my pack today. You aren't at all who I thought you were."

"I don't even know who I am anymore," she said. She turned in his arms to look up into his eyes, which were glowing in the late afternoon sun. "Why do you keep kissing me?"

"It's just instinctual. Especially because I want you to know you'll be mine."

"That's impossible," she said. "I'm tribunal, and you're—"

"A mongrel, I know."

"Wonderful," she said. "Honest. Loyal. Nothing like the world I came from. I should go back there. Keep trouble from following me here."

He shook his head. "I'd never let you."

"Because you owe me?" she asked.

"That, and because I can't let you go now. I physically can't let you go."

"That makes no sense."

"I don't have to make sense," he said with a wry smile. "I'm a wolf."

She sighed and took a step back, out of his arms. "I don't know what will happen next. I can't promise you anything. All I can do is make the best decisions I can as this unfolds. There's no protocol for what is happening to me, and I have no way to know their decision. If they come for me, I can't promise I won't go, if it means you and your pack are safe."

He took a step forward, tall and intimidating. "If they took you, I'd come for you."

Somehow she didn't doubt him. "If you came for me, it would be too late."

"I don't care," he said, closing the distance. "You've always been in my mind, even when I knew it was hopeless."

She turned to look at him. "Really?"

His gaze was earnest. Sincere. "Yes. And when you came here, when you slept in that chair that first night, and I kept watch, I couldn't help thinking you were beautiful. I wanted to touch you."

"Hm," she said, vaguely unnerved, but still a little turned on. Why was it that things that would have pissed her off if other males did them, turned her on when he did them?

"You were everything I wanted to be, so I was blinded by my jealousy. But I have to say the jealousy I felt when I thought I had to compete with you is nothing compared to the jealousy of watching another wolf touch you. Male or female."

She swallowed.

"So you may be worried about my pack. You may want me to let you walk away when the time comes. But I promise you that isn't an option anymore. My body will fight to the last breath for you, even if you reject me. So you'll just have to accept that I'm strong enough to protect you *and* the pack."

She just continued staring, her whole body hot at the pure alpha strength he was exuding at this moment.

"Your wolf brought you to me in a moment of instinct," he continued. "Now you have to trust me to take care of you." He gave her a cocky grin ad walked past her to the cabin, leaving her cold and wanting.

Her features tightened in anger. How could he make a speech like that, one that rocked her to her core, and just leave? Hell no! She stomped after him, caught up, and jerked on his arm so he'd face her. Then she launched up on her toes, threw her arms around his neck and stole his mouth with hers.

His stupid, romantic babble had made her whole world fall apart.

His shock quickly turned to surprise as he ran his hands along her body. He growled and deepened the kiss, stroking inside her mouth and thrusting against her tongue with an intensity that set her to burning nearly instantly.

They were like steel and flint, ready to spark at any moment and burn into a blaze that could obliterate everything around them.

There had never been anyone else for either of them, so the intensity of years was pouring out all in these few moments. He lifted her off her toes as he crushed her to him. She felt safe, warm and wanted. She felt like a true female for the first time in her life. When they'd made out before, it had felt heavenly, but new and confusing. It had almost felt like it was happening to someone else.

But right now it just felt perfect.

She growled against his mouth and tried to press herself closer to him. He caught her under her butt and lifted her to his waist and she wrapped her legs around him, growling and kissing him as he walked easily toward the cabin. He carried her like she was nothing compared to him, and she was not a short female.

She dug her hands into the short, thick hair that was a gorgeous blackened brown in the shade, and a black-cherry auburn in the sunlight. So thick, so strong, like him. Harsh, masculine, but different and unique.

She broke the kiss and leaned back to catch her breath and he turned his attention to her neck, laving and licking and biting as she dug her nails into his shoulders and back.

She didn't know what would happen when they reached the cabin, but she knew it was going to be good. She didn't much care beyond that. Her wolf was in control, howling at the moon, happy to have found her mate.

Mate. The word thudded through her, leaving ripples like a stone thrown in a pond. She held onto him tighter, savoring the feel of his lips, the heat he was building in her.

She could think of the difficult things later. Just once, she deserved to have fun.

And he wanted to mate her anyway, so what was the problem? They were two strong alphas, they could weather any storm.

She felt him stop and heard a familiar voice clear its throat. She felt Thor freeze against her. He slowly set her beside him on the ground, and then put an arm out in front of her. She could feel his body, so tense, so still. She took a deep breath and glanced up at the cabin to see what was bothering him.

Her eyes widened.

She hadn't known what to expect when they got to the house, but this was the last thing she'd expected.

The door was open, and Thor's twin Lock, who'd been missing for years, was standing in the doorway.

CHAPTER 10

Lock looked a lot like she'd remembered. She looked from him to Thor and once again noted the difference. Thor was muscled, kind of stiff, and had an abundance of severe alpha-ness when he wanted to. His hair was short, athletic, and he wore practical, masculine clothing that wouldn't get in the way.

Lock had longer hair, but it was the same color as Thor's since they were identical. His face was relaxed, as usual, but unlike Thor who was easy to read, there always seemed to be something under the surface with Lock.

She didn't know what to make of him. She knew he'd kidnapped Misty during an alpha challenge and then changed his mind and gotten shot saving her life. But she didn't know much else about him, except that he'd made his brother supplicate himself on the ground to save his life.

Lock preferred leather and distressed tee shirts. Bracelets and little braids. His hair was feathered around his face and collar. He was a much softer version of Thor, unless you looked in those eyes. If Thor's eyes were warm brandy, Lock's were frozen amber.

"Long time no see," Lock said quietly.

She felt Thor take a deep breath. She knew how much he must care about him, judging by what he'd gone through before.

She felt Lock's eyes on her for the first time, and he gave her a quick once over. Something like disgust flared in his eyes and she flinched, but convinced herself to stand tall.

"What's she doing here?" he asked Thor. "Fraternizing with the enemy now, are we? And yes, I know Matt's a she."

Her heart was still pounding from the kiss, from Thor's ownership of her body. It was exactly the wrong time to meet up with his long-lost, pissy twin. Who somehow knew her secret.

Lock pushed off the doorframe and took a couple lazy steps forward. Thor stepped slightly in front of her.

"She needs help," he said. "She came to me because I owed her. You know, for…"

Lock sneered. "Ah yes, for having to kneel to the tribunal to save my ass. Got it." Lock stepped off the porch and circled them, making her uneasy. There was such thinly veiled anger surging through him that she didn't know what to make of it, but she stayed close to Thor.

Even Thor seemed confused by his brother's hate. "I've never known you to not want to help someone."

Lock raised an eyebrow. "Really? Well, maybe that's changed now that I know who murdered our parents. Maybe I don't like finally making it back here to tell you only to find out you're sleeping with their fucking daughter!"

And with that, Lock turned on his heel and marched into the house, slamming the door behind him.

Her heart slammed into her throat. It couldn't be true. Thor turned to her with wounded eyes, and she took a step back.

"It's not true, it can't be."

Thor shook his head and walked into the house. She hesitated, and he turned back. "You coming?"

She twisted her shirt in her hands. "I don't know if I should."

He bit his lip. "You're the one I want for my mate. Whatever he says won't change that. Why don't you wait in your room while I talk to him?"

She shook her head. "No, if this has to do with me, then I want to hear it. I deserve to hear it. I'm not afraid of his anger."

"You have no need to be. I'm with you," he said.

Her heart warmed at the words, but she still felt cold fear at what waited for her inside the cabin. Not the anger of Thor's brother, but the truth of what her family could be capable of. "I know. But he's your brother."

"And I've been handling him for years. I know him, Matt. He's angry, so am I. We've been waiting for years to know what happened. So please, be patient with him."

"I will be," she said.

"I can't promise he won't say things that are hurtful."

"He won't be the first. And if what he says is true, I'll agree with him. I'll help him avenge them myself."

Thor sighed. "Well, let's see just what's going on first." He put out an arm and she took it and walked with him into the cabin.

***

The wood creaked as they walked over the threshold. Thor flicked on a switch and Lock was illuminated at the kitchen table, sitting hunched over a cup of something to drink, hair hanging down and shadowing his face. He was a handsome wolf, like his brother, but he was clearly only barely hanging on to his sense of civilization. She could sense that the wolf in him was desperate to break out. For vengeance.

His cold eyes flicked to her as they walked closer, as if he'd scented her. He let out a low snarl and Thor stepped in front of her to block her from view.

"Lock, this doesn't involve her. She's not with the tribunal anymore."

Lock shoved his hand across the table, knocking the glass to the ground with a loud smash. He stood and grabbed Thor by the collar. "Was she involved when they killed our parents? When they killed Misty's parents? When they created a false scarcity of alpha females so that we would all have to fight to even breed with one?" Thor remained calm and Lock released him. "Has she told you about any of that?"

"Calm yourself," Thor said, watching Lock warily as he paced. "No, she hasn't. But I assume that means it's because she wasn't part of it. Maybe you should let Matt tell you her story before you go off making assumptions."

Lock turned to him, a grimace of disgust plain on his handsome face. "Why? Because you want an alpha female so much that you'd forget the fact that you used to hate her? You'd believe her lies instantly? I've protected you for a long time, Thor, but how could you be so naive?"

This time Thor grabbed Lock by the collar and hauled him up so they were nose to nose. "Protected me? Is that what you call it? Getting in with the wrong group? Nearly getting executed? Making me save your butt and then disappearing on me for years? Is that what you call brotherhood?" He released Lock and shoved him away from him. "I don't know you anymore."

Lock rested his hands on his knees, and Matt realized he was trembling slightly. He must be hungry. Who knew how far he had come. She saw him waver on his feet and ran to put herself under his arm to catch him as he fell forward. She looked up at Thor, who stared at her in shock as she helped Lock over to the nearest chair and sat him in it. Then she got up and went to the fridge.

"You must be hungry," she called over her shoulder.

Lock muttered something that sounded like "hungry for vengeance", but she ignored it and pulled together some deli meat and vegetables. Thor sighed and handed her a plate and she put everything on it and put it in front of Lock.

He dug into it, eating more like a wolf than a human. Thor eyed her warily, as if he couldn't decide if he should be mad at her for interfering or grateful that she was taking care of his brother. Thor sat in a chair next to Lock while he ate.

"I should have asked if you were hungry," he said.

Lock shrugged his massive shoulders. "I intruded. Anger was carrying me where food never could. I've been angry a long time, Thor. They took everything. Do you know how our lives could have been? Instead…" He shook his head. "But it's too late. But they'll pay. Oh yes, they'll pay. Just as soon as I figure out how."

Matt settled in a chair near the kitchen so she could watch.

Lock flicked his gaze at her and then back to Thor. He grinned. "At least you figured out she was a female. How did you do it, with all the technology they keep for themselves and not us?"

Thor shook his head. "I walked in on her changing."

Lock raised an eyebrow. "Seriously?" He laughed. He sounded more like the Lock she remembered when he laughed. "Good for you."

"Good for me?" Thor asked, voice dark and growly.

"Yes," Lock said. "Since I'm sure the little bitch wasn't going to tell you her secret."

Thor stood, pushing out his chair. "Don't call her that."

"Bitch, female wolf. Come on, Thor, don't be touchy."

Thor sat. "Nevertheless, don't call her that. She's going to be my mate."

A bitter smile quirked one side of Lock's full lips. "Oh is she? Really? You think a top member of the tribunal family is really going to pick you? How do you know she's not just spying on you? Using you, waiting for what she needs and then ready to turn on you at any second."

Matt crossed the room. She'd heard enough. She grabbed Lock by the collar and looked straight into his eyes. He stayed relaxed but anger burned in his amber gaze.

"That's enough," she said. "You don't know me. You just think you do. So maybe you should calm down until you know who to accuse."

He looked her up and down. "Maybe. Or maybe I've just found a way to get back at the tribunal." He yanked her against him, arm around her waist, and she gasped and tried to free herself. A second later, she found herself plucked from his grasp and tossed backwards by an angry Thor, who was now transforming into a wolf to face his brother, who was transforming as well.

Their wolves were dark reddish-brown and huge because they were pure alphas. They growled as they circled. She could tell which one was Thor because his fur was slightly shorter. And because she knew his scent and his posture.

"You would defend her against me? Your blood?" Lock asked, disdain in his voice. "This is what the tribunal has wrought. A desperation for alpha females that turns brother against brother, alpha against alpha. Meanwhile we are so busy fighting each other that we don't know what they are doing."

"And what are they doing?" Thor snarled back. "Because I'm not going to let you hurt an innocent female, regardless of your suppositions."

"Not suppositions, brother. *Facts.* And I paid dearly for them, so don't tell me that I don't know what I'm talking about."

Thor circled his brother. "Then explain. But do it without harming the person I'm supposed to be protecting."

"I wasn't going to harm her," he said. "I was just going to *taste* her."

Thor growled and lunged toward his brother and they clashed in a tangle of fur and teeth. Matt rolled her eyes and transformed into wolf form. She jumped between them and focused and a bubble of energy burst around her, knocking them back on either side, sending them sprawling against either wall.

They sat up and looked at her in shock.

She lowered her head and fought the crackling pain surging through her. She lowered herself to the ground, head between her paws, and waited for the pain to abate.

"What the hell was that?" Thor asked, limping toward her. "I feel weak as a kitten."

"Where are my alpha powers?" Lock asked, shaking one of his paws. "What the hell did you just do to me?"

She grinned at them warily as she felt herself begin to transform. "That's my alpha ability. That probably only makes you more pissed at me and my family, but my alpha power can temporarily negate yours." Her body spasmed and shook and she fought the transformation so she could get to her feet. She limped toward her room. "So now you two have to work it out like brothers. With your brains instead of your fists." She made it to the room and shut the door behind her, and then plopped down and transformed back into a human.

She let out a sigh of relief.

"Matt? Lacey? You okay?" Thor called.

"I'm fine," she said. "I just need to recover. Talk to your brother."

Then she fell asleep, naked, on the ground.

CHAPTER 11

Thor eyed his brother warily as they both slowly changed, weak from transforming and whatever it was Matt had done to them. He'd never felt anything like it. Pure force, and then a feeling like the circuits in his body weren't working.

"Lock?" he asked as he buttoned his jeans.

"Yes?" Lock replied, buttoning his own. Sometimes looking at his brother was like looking in a mirror.

"It's good to see you," Thor said, throat tight from some unknown emotion. He'd known Lock had to be out there somewhere, because they'd had a link since birth that when the other was badly wounded, they knew.

When Lock had been shot helping Misty back at the mansion, Thor had felt the bullet tear through his body and sheer panic had engulfed him.

He'd felt like he was going to die.

Lock gave him a guilty look as he slumped into a chair. "I know I should have come back sooner. I was still figuring things out. And I didn't want you in danger again."

"If you're in danger, I'm in danger," Thor said, folding his arms and taking a chair across from his brother.

Lock looked well. His hair was a little unkempt, a little longer than usual, and there were a few stress lines around his eyes that would probably resolve with a little sleep and some good food, but all in all, he seemed healthy.

"Where have you been?" he asked. "And what has happened since I've seen you?"

Lock let out a hoarse laugh that was more like a bark. "What hasn't happened?"

"You know what I mean."

Lock sighed, a rough exhale of breath that made Thor think his brother hadn't had a chance to relax in a long time. "You know how I was caught, right?"

Thor shook his head. "It was actually Fifi who even let me know you were in trouble. He didn't have the power to do anything about it, but he told me to go to Matt. Said he could." He scrubbed his hands through his hair. "That's back when I thought Matt was a boy."

"Fifi, hm? I thought he might have interfered." Lock sighed and got a cryptic expression that Thor couldn't read. "And as for Matt, even as a boy she kind of got under your skin, didn't she?" Lock asked, a teasing gleam in his eyes. "I guess she can't be all bad. She did turn on her family to let me go."

He sighed and put his face in his hands, slowly pulling them down, stretching his skin. Then he sat up. "I've gone and done it now. It's just, I've been preparing myself to come tell you what I know, knowing how angry it'll make you. How angry it has made me. And then I see you, with her legs wrapped around your waist. Carrying her like it never occurred to you there could be something wrong with it."

Thor nodded. "I know."

"And then, it's like, it was always us, you know? Somehow I thought I'd come back and we'd go back to the way things were, fighting the man, trying to win our way in the world. But now you have this cabin and the pack back. Was everything I did for nothing?"

Lock looked up at the ceiling like it had the answers he was looking for, and then looked back at Thor. "I can't unlearn what I know, and that kills me. Because all I wanted was for you to be happy, and now I don't see how that can happen."

"What do you mean?" Thor asked, a dark feeling in the pit of his stomach.

"I guess I'll tell you what I know and we'll take it from there," Lock said.

"She hasn't agreed to be my mate," Thor said. "Just so you know. Nothing is final. But she's on the run from the tribunal and she came to me, and I'm attracted to her, and the pack needs an alpha female, so why not? But nothing is set in stone yet."

Lock nodded. "I know, I could scent it when she was close. I don't know what came over me. I wanted to hurt them like they hurt me. So I grabbed her. But you know I wouldn't have done anything."

Thor bit his lip and eyed his brother. Did he know that? He thought he did, but this brother was new to him. Knew things he didn't. Showed anger like he never had before.

Growing up the way they had had been hard on both of them, but he'd never seen that in Lock until he'd started to cross the line.

He was seeing it now. "What did you find out?"

Lock shook his head. "Not here. Let's go outside. I don't know how much she knows, but I'm not saying more just in case. If she's a spy, I don't need her tipping them off."

"She's not a spy," Thor said. "She's as scared of them as you are."

"I'm not scared of them," Lock spat out. "I'm disgusted by them. There's a difference. Nevertheless, I'm not talking in front of her. If you can't keep a secret, then I'm not telling you anything either. Your choice. I can deal with this on my own."

Thor's heart clenched. This was his blood, his twin, part of him. He didn't want to keep Matt out of the loop, but until she was his mate, she didn't come before his family. "Fine," he said. "Tell me what you know, and I won't tell her until you've had time to see that she's on our side. Although it seems like you've already blurted out most of it anyway."

"Fine," Lock said. "Now walk outside with me. I'd like a chance to see how the grounds look anyway."

Thor nodded and led his brother outside, dread circling inside him like water circling a drain. All his life he'd wanted to know what happened to his parents. Why he'd grown up the way he had. But suddenly, he wasn't so eager anymore.

Suddenly, he was wondering if it was better if he didn't know.

***

When Matt woke up, soft evening light was filtering through the slits in her drapes. She pulled herself off the ground and stumbled to her bag to look for clothes. She sat on the bed and started to wrap her chest wearily, the action pure habit after doing it for so many years. Even though the two wolves nearby knew her secret, there was no telling who else might come by.

A soft knock sounded on her door and she stood, stretching as she pulled on a shirt and some pajama pants. "Coming."

"It's Thor," the voice said.

She opened the door and looked him up and down. Damn, he was a sight for sore eyes. "How did it go?" she asked. "With your brother, I mean."

"He's out in the woods right now," he said. "Running it off. It's probably safer for him there. Less likely to be spotted."

She nodded. "Especially since they might have scouts out looking for me by now."

Thor nodded. "Can I come in?"

She opened the door wider and swept a hand in welcome. "Of course. It's your home. What did he say?"

Now that they were alone, she could feel the heat rising again. Remember how it felt when her legs had been wrapped around his waist when he'd been carrying her to the cabin. How promising that had been.

Thor hesitated. He ran a hand through his short hair, mussing it further, and from the many tortured directions it was sticking in, she guessed he'd been doing that a lot since she last saw him.

"How long was I out?" she asked.

"A few hours," he said. "When I heard rustling, I knocked. Other than that, I thought you needed space. What was that you did to me and my brother?"

She shrugged. "My alpha ability," she said. "Unfortunately, it renders me as helpless as the people I use it on. It's part of why my father sent me to alpha challenges. He said it was to make sure no alphas killed each other. But after what your brother said, and after he turned on me, who knows what's really true?"

"Matt, what my brother told me. He told me not to tell you. Not until he's ready to trust you."

She frowned, feeling a tightness in her chest that she didn't like. "And you agreed? You're going to keep secrets from me?"

"You have secrets too, don't you?" he asked. "They aren't my secrets to keep. And Lock has been gone for years, waiting to find them and tell me.

And they are about my parents, not yours."

"Or both?" she guessed. "He said my parents were involved."

"That's part of it," he agreed. "But yeah, I can't tell you everything. I can tell you this though. None of this changes anything for me. I want to mate you, tribunal or not. I want you to join my pack. I want you for my own. I won't let anyone take you."

"That's nice and all, but you don't really trust me, do you? Or you'd tell me."

"Have you told me everything you know about the tribunal?" he asked.

She sucked in her cheeks. What she knew about the tribunal could fill a small book. But what she didn't know could probably fill a much larger one.

"I thought so," he said, suspicion lighting his gaze. "Anyway, we don't have to know everything about each other to mate."

"But can we really keep secrets from each other?" she asked.

"I don't see how we can't. When Lock is won over, then I can tell you. Until then, can you put it out of your head?"

"Can you?" she asked. "If you truly think my parents murdered yours, can you really be with me? Can you really look at me and not see them? Are you sure you wouldn't grow to hate me?"

He sat in the chair by her bed and looked out the window. "You know, Lock and I are different. I guess I gave up on finding out about my parents long ago. I had my rebellious phase, my hating the world phase, my wanting everyone to pay phase. And then I came back here, inherited the money my parents wanted us to use to take care of the pack. With my brother gone, I was the obvious choice as alpha, and I found meaning here in ousting my uncle and trying to repair the lives he damaged. It wasn't only my life he ruined. And that need to help others has been consuming my life, while revenge has been consuming Lock's."

She nodded.

"I'm hoping one day Lock finds something that means more to him than revenge. Because I have."

She flushed, and then realized he might not be talking about her. "You mean the pack?"

He nodded. "Yes. They need me."

"Oh." For a minute she'd thought he meant her, and that would have been wonderful. Even if it made no sense.

"But you as well. With you, I can rebuild more than I ever have before."

"So it's just for the pack, then?" she asked. "It's just so that I can help you rebuild?"

He let out a long, exasperated sigh. "We keep coming back to that. No. If I wanted to hunt down an alpha female, I would have left the pack and done it. But none had ever interested me."

"Maybe you just weren't in the right place yet."

"No," he said. "Don't you see? You're the key. You came at just the right time. You need me as much as I need you. And we've known each other, fought each other, and helped each other for a long time."

She sighed. "I know."

He captured her chin in his hand and kept her gaze. "Some cultures believe in a red thread of fate that binds us to our soul mate. The longer I'm with you, the more I know. You are my red thread mate."

She swallowed. It was the most romantic thing she'd ever heard. And it made sense. They kept meeting up. Kept finding each other, kept needing each other.

Perhaps there really was something like destiny pulling them together.

But did that mean that nothing could pull them apart?

He reached for her, pulling her onto his lap in the chair. Despite the complications between them, she couldn't resist. She'd never been romanced before. Never been attracted like this before. And his big, hard body felt so right beneath hers.

Whether they could officially mate or not, she wanted to be with him.

"When will your brother be back?" she asked quietly, reaching up to play with an errant spike of hair.

"Late," he said. "He's not spending the night in the house."

"Are you sure that what he told you didn't change things?" she asked.

"Positive," he said. "I'm not going to let the past determine my future. Lock knows this."

"Then what will you do?" she asked. There was a husky note in her voice. Sitting there together now, with Lock and his secrets out of the way, and Thor having just talked about destiny, it was almost as if the disruption in the afternoon hadn't happened. As if no one had interrupted them while he carried her to the cabin.

"I'll take it one thing at a time. And right now, I want to take the she-wolf that I feel has been destined for me."

"Not as mate," she said. "Not yet."

"Just let me make love to you," he said. "And we can decide on the rest later."

"Hell yes," she murmured, as he pushed her hair back from her ear and stroked a finger along the delicate inner shell. She shivered. "The rest can come later."

He picked her up in his arms and carried her to the bed. They locked eyes for a moment, an electric current running between them, and then he set her down gently in the center of the covers.

Who knew what tomorrow would bring? But right now, she'd enjoy everything that it seemed the universe had intended.

Just for one night, she'd enjoy all the pleasure he had to give.

CHAPTER 12

Thor felt her body under his hands, needing to reassure himself that she was here, she was his.

"Are you sure?" he asked.

"I should be asking you that," she said.

"I've been sure from the moment I found out you were female. And if I'd found out sooner, I would have been sure before that."

"Oh," she said.

"And when you were male, you were just confusing," he said.

She giggled and then paused, her eyes wide. "What did I just do?"

"Why Matt, I think you just giggled," he said, teasing as he played with the edge of her shirt, threatening to lift it.

"I did not," she said. "Call me Lacey."

"No," he said. "I like Matt."

"You want to have sex with a girl named Matt?"

"No," he said, easing the shirt up and grabbing the edge of her breast bindings gently with his teeth. He tugged them loose and then brought up his hands to unwind them. She arched to make it easier.

"I want to mate with a girl named Matt. I want to grow old with a girl named Matt. I want to have babies with a girl named Matt."

"But you hated me when I was Matt," she said.

"And fate knew better than I did," he said. "At least I always noticed you."

She nodded, a pretty flush filling her cheeks as she looked down and saw that she was nearly bared to him. "Thor…"

"What?" he asked.

"When do you think Lock will trust me?" she asked. "I mean, maybe he's right. Maybe you shouldn't be trusting me."

"Right now, you're the one trusting me. In fact, you're giving me the most trust one being can give another." He looked down at her body, naked from the waist up, and hooked his fingers into the waistband of her pants. "You're letting me make love to you, being fully vulnerable."

"I think there are worse ways to be vulnerable," she said, as he pulled down her pants and played with the top of her lace underwear.

"Lacey," he said.

"Yes?" she said.

"No, these. Lacey," he said, grinning. They were so light, so delicate. Nothing like the hard female alpha wolf he'd gotten to know. But in these moments, he saw the vulnerable side of her, the soft side. In these moments, he'd never let anyone hurt her.

Blue eyes looked up to his and blinked rapidly. "Thor..."

"Yes?" he asked, toying with the edges of her panties, excited to pull them off.

"Give me everything."

"What?" he asked. "I thought you didn't want..."

"I want," she said. "But use protection."

"Ah, everything but mating."

"Yes, but I want you to make love to me."

"I can do that," he said, feeling only slightly bitter that he couldn't go all the way and make her his right now. "I'd rather do more, but I can do that."

Her body was prettily flushed, the tips of her nipples dusky and erect. She covered herself with her hands and he pulled them to the side and kissed the top of each breast lightly. She quivered beneath him, biting her lip, and the sight drove him to near madness.

He tore the panties off and tossed them to the side of the bed. She tried to sit up but he pushed her back on the bed. "Not so fast, princess."

"Bully," she grumbled, but she lay back and let him climb on top of her. He was still fully clothed, and he could tell from the way she eyed his body that she'd liked that rectified. He gave her a wink and then reached for the bottom of his shirt and lifted it slowly over his head, giving her a view of the body he'd sculpted through years of work. He was an alpha male, and his body was all hers. These muscles would protect her. These hands would hold her.

And nothing anyone told him could change that. His wolf had decided that. And his wolf had led him to the only happiness he'd had so far, so he was going to listen to it.

He tossed his shirt and then reached for his jeans buttons. She bit her lip and exhaled slowly as he undid the button and slid the zipper down. She lifted a fist to her mouth and bit down slightly, and the knowledge that he was driving her as crazy as she was driving him made him hard as a rock. He shifted as he lowered the zipper, but then stopped, leaving it only slightly undone.

She was writhing slightly beneath him, and despite promising her he would give her what she wanted, he found himself wanting to give her a little something else first.

He cupped her face in his hands, savoring the wonder there, and then moved down her body, letting his hands make a searing trail over her as he knelt between her legs. Then, before she could say anything about it, he hefted her legs up so that her knees were over his shoulders, his hands on her thighs. His mouth…just where he wanted it to be.

He flicked his tongue out and she gasped and jerked, but was held completely by him. He looked down her lean body and saw her breasts, peaked and sheened in sweat, and her face, shocked but quickly being taken over by pleasure.

He licked out again, feeling up the center of her to the place where she jerked most intensely, the spot where all the pleasure was centered. He kissed it gently and she moaned and put her hands up in her hair, dragging her fingers through it.

"Thor, what are you—?" Her words cut off in a gasp as he sucked gently and then grazed her ever so lightly with his teeth, testing the pressure she liked best. He wanted to know everything about how to please her. He wanted to see her come apart in his arms an unlimited amount of times. Nothing else mattered but that.

She cried out his name as he kept her trapped against his mouth. Her scent, her taste, was amazing. Sweet, heady, his. He knew he could stay there all day, but he could tell from her breathing and the frantic movements of her body that she was close to losing it. All the better. He'd make sure she lost it a few times so that she was good and relaxed when he entered her and gave her what she wanted. She was tight, and this would be her first time, so he'd need to be careful.

At least, that was his excuse for lingering here at this most delightful place, watching her writhe and scream. He sensed she was just about there, so he reached out to splay a hand over her belly, running a thumb gently over her navel as his lips sucked and his tongue pressed down firmly.

She came, face darkening with pleasure as she curled up slightly and then threw her head back in an arch, calling his name and moaning with pleasure. He held her legs but lowered slightly so she was comfortable, but she didn't seem to notice, bucking against him as each wave of pleasure hit.

"Again?" he asked.

"Oh gosh," she gasped out. "Seriously? Is that even possible—?" She caught her breath as he started again. He'd show her just how possible it was. Over and over.

***

His hands on her thighs. His gaze on her body as his tongue licked her wickedly, teasing and torturing her in the most sensitive of places. He was a bully through and through. She'd asked for one thing and he'd given her another. But it was so wonderful, so freaking amazing, that she thought she'd probably forgive him this time.

Her body was lifted in front of her, helpless and pleasured, and as he started that slow, nearly painful build again, she didn't know how she could handle it. But she also didn't know how she could handle it if he didn't keep going.

Was this really Thornton Wilder doing this to her now? The thought was hot but incomprehensible. But even back when they'd clashed, she'd be lying if she said she'd never fantasized about him using his strength on her in other ways.

Not that she had considered him as mate. She'd always known she couldn't have a mate. But she'd thought of him. Yes, of those brandy eyes and that amazing body, and that thick hair she wanted to put her hands in. Maybe next time she could be on top, touching him as she liked. But for now, letting him hold her, pleasure her until she was half out of her mind, would do just fine.

"Thor," she said. "Thor, Thor, Thor." She tossed her head from side to side, murmuring his name like she couldn't help it. It was like she almost wanted to ask him to stop, but then wanted to ask him to never stop, and then just wanted to ask him to do even more.

Instead, she just said his name.

Each time she did, his eyes met hers, pleased, and his tongue stroked and laved again, kissing her wickedly, holding her captive, keeping her pleasure rising at his own pace. Her body was reacting on its own, and her wolf was contented and purring within her. It felt amazing. She felt another crescendo coming and ran her own hand over her stomach, the way he had done. He reached for her and took her hand. Then he kept his hot eyes on her, long lashes lowered, and gave her a kiss to beat all of the others.

She swirled over the brink and into a free fall of pleasure. She barely heard her own scream, and tried to stifle it when she did.

She couldn't stop what was happening inside her and she didn't want to. She raised a fist to her mouth and bit lightly down on it. But then he was releasing her, letting her legs finally fall to the bedspread as he gathered her in his arms. He gave her a kiss and she tasted herself on his lips. Tasted their scents together, felt his tongue slide into her mouth and love her and muffle her cries as she rode out her orgasm.

His bare, sweat-sheened chest to hers felt amazing. She never wanted them to separate. They were one. He pulled back from the kiss and trailed a finger down from her breast to her navel to between her legs, feeling and testing, and then he put his finger to his mouth and slowly licked.

Damn, that made her hot.

"Take me," she said, writhing and clenching her legs together against the ache rising between them. "Take me, Thor."

He nodded. "Soon." He made as if to raise her legs to his shoulders again, and she put her hands on his arms and stopped him with a growl.

"No, *now*," she said.

"Princess?" he asked, holding her hands, a battle of wills raging between them.

"Yes?" she replied.

"I'm in charge." He ran his hands in a tingling line down her legs, all the way to her ankles and then her toes. Everywhere he touched felt naughty. Everywhere he touched felt amazing.

"You're in charge," she said huskily, biting the inside of her cheek as he started to haul her legs up on either side of his head again. He was about to kiss her, when she locked her thighs on either side of his head, crossed her legs, and jerked him forward.

He stumbled and caught himself on both hands over her, and she found the shocked look in his eyes sexy as hell. She slid her legs off his shoulders and rolled out from under him and off the bed. He looked up at her, perplexed, and then a predatory gleam lit his eyes and he started to get off the bed.

The thrill of the chase ran through her, but she grabbed her wrist wraps and held them behind her back as she lunged back to the bed to knock him on his back. He landed in a huff and before he could recover, she had the wraps looped around one wrist and then over the bed frame.

He raised an eyebrow and looked from his hand to the bed. Then he yanked on it, expecting it to break. But those were some tough wraps. She grinned and his eyes narrowed as she reached for his other hand.

"Don't you dare," he said.

But she just laughed and captured the other hand in record time and tied that one to the bed frame as well. Before long his tall, muscular body was displayed below her, his arms tensing as he tested the bonds, his expression dark as he struggled with the fact that he wasn't in charge.

"Your turn," she said quietly, running a finger down his chest, between his massive, cut pectorals, over the deep ridges of his abs. She stopped at his belly button and he sucked in a ragged breath.

"Let me go," he said. "I want to please you."

She looked up at him, pleasure gleaming in her eyes. "You are." Then she reached for the zipper of his pants and slowly pulled it down. He groaned as his member sprung free into her hands. She touched it in wonder. It was softer than she had thought, the skin there like velvet. But it was hard as she tested its strength in her hands. And huge. Could it possibly fit?

She shrugged and continued running her hands up and down the length.

"Let me go," he growled, testing the bonds. She heard the bed frame creak but didn't care. He'd dominated her, made her completely helpless with pleasure, and she intended to return the favor. She leaned forward and licked slowly up the side of his cock. He jerked against her, eyes bulging in shock.

"Damn that feels good," he groaned. "Don't stop."

She grinned. She kissed the tip of him and then tried putting him in her mouth. He was too big, but she still enjoyed the feel of it. More than that, she enjoyed his harsh little pants of breath, the way his incredible body tensed under hers. He was used to being in control, taking care of everything, and it was the ultimate power trip to see this powerful alpha completely at her mercy.

She removed her lips from him and moved up to sit on his stomach so she could trace the shape of his pecs, draw around the indentations in his abdomen. He caught his breath.

"You're torturing me. Let me go, and I'll end it for both of us," he said.

She shook her head, waggling a finger. "Nope. Right now, I'm in charge." She reached up along his bulging arms, cupping his massive biceps. She felt his abs tense beneath her. If he wasn't tied right now, she'd be powerless to him. She stroked a finger along his cut jaw, and he nipped at it with his teeth. She pulled back, laughing. "Oh come on, turnabout is fair play."

"You liked my turnabout and you know it," he griped.

She turned to look at his hard dick, still standing at attention. "And you seem to like mine."

"I like that you want me," he said, looking at her with eyes hot enough to boil. "But I'd like it even more if I could show you just how much I want you back."

"You did," she said, tracing the arc of his full upper lip carefully. "But if you want me for a mate, you're going to have to accept that I'm going to be in charge at least some of the time. I am an alpha female, after all."

He gritted his teeth and she loved the little flex in his jaw when he did it. "I don't know, princess. But I look forward to seeing how it works out."

"Who knows?" she said, tracing down his arms again and moving back to take his hard member in her hand. "But right now, I just want to experience you."

"You're torturing me," he said, when she leaned forward to kiss it again. "Damn, you're so innocent."

"Maybe," she said. "But I think you like it." She blew on the wet tip of his penis and he arched, biting his lip.

"Stop that," he said. "You can't foreplay with me like I can with you. There's only one feeling my body wants, princess. Me, deep inside you."

"That's not all you seemed to want a moment ago."

"That's the only feeling I want, not the only feeling I want you to want. I want to watch you lose it over and over again, until you're wet and ready and aching down there for me to take you. Then I want you to come again a few times, until you're practically begging. And then when I do take you, I want it to be the answer to a prayer. The culmination of hours of aching. I want it to be everything, princess."

She ached at that and writhed uncomfortably, suddenly wanting him free so he could fulfill all of the promises he'd been making. "I'm ready for you now," she said. "If I untied you, would you promise to stop torturing me?"

"Never," he said, eyes gleaming.

"Then I can't let you go," she said regretfully, hating how her body was aching for him. Having him tied was her only bargaining chip.

"That's okay," he said, jerking forward suddenly, her torn wraps falling from his hands. "I'm an alpha male, so I'll make do."

"What?" she asked, gasping as he gripped her hips and lifted her onto his waist again, holding her tightly to him.

He grinned. "Oh come on, I let you have some fun. I could tell it was getting you off. But the moment you wanted me in control again, my wolf made it happen. I'm an alpha male, Princess," he said, looking at the bed frame and shaking his hands. "You had to know you couldn't really restrain me if I didn't want you to."

She blushed, but didn't care anymore as his hands moved up to capture her breasts. He tweaked the nipples and fire surged through her, bringing her to life in new places every moment. "Thor," she said. "Take me."

He growled. "Normally I'd want to go longer just pleasuring you, but after that little torture session a moment ago, I don't think I can wait any longer. So I guess you're getting what you wanted." He opened a drawer in the bed stand and pulled open a condom, ripped it open, and moved her back so he could slide it on. Then he slid his hand between her legs.

"Good, you're wet and ready for me. It's your first time, so I'll try not to hurt you, Princess."

"I'm nobody's princess anymore," she said, rubbing against him.

"Then be my queen," he said. Then he lifted her and slid into her with one firm thrust.

She gasped and winced as her hips met his stomach, the two of them sealed as one. Her body tensed and she made as if to lift herself, and then relaxed as she felt the pressure turn from slight pain to immense pleasure. "That's…it's…"

"Is it okay?" he asked, shifting slightly.

She nodded, planting her hands on his chest and leaning forward slightly to change the angle between them. She shut her eyes tight and swallowed. Then she bit her lip. "It feels… so good. I didn't know…" She bit her lip again. "Oh gosh, Thor. It's perfect. You fit perfectly inside me. It was so tight at first, I didn't know how, and then…"

He watched her, heat rising in him as her breathing increased. It took all of his self-control not to start moving until she was ready.

Apparently she was ready, because she started to move on top of him. Lifting up slightly and then setting herself over him again. Delicious friction washed over him and she did it again. Another slow, torturous inch. Another widening of her eyes and gasp from her perfect lips.

She was going to kill him.

"I'm sorry, princess," he said. "But I'm going to need to take this one."

"What?" she asked, lips parted.

In answer, he rolled her under him.

CHAPTER 13

She gasped at finding herself on the bottom, but was slightly relieved. Aside from the delicious tension of having him inside her, she wasn't sure what else to do. She was ready for him, her body was ready, but she didn't know what to do to bring them to completion.

Luckily, he seemed more than happy to make that *his* job.

He looked down into her eyes and ran his tongue swiftly over his lower lip. Then he leaned in to kiss her, taking her mouth deeply, swirling his tongue inside her as he began to move.

She gasped as he slowly pulled nearly all the way out, leaving her empty, and then slid back in, hilt deep. Her whole body felt electrified by the contact, as if there was a void in her that had never been filled until that moment. Just as she adjusted, he pulled out again, this time a little faster, and then thrust quickly back inside. The sensation was even stronger and she arched against it, her hands twisting in the sheets around them.

She panted as he continued to stroke. The feeling was incomparable, but it was more than that. His face, strong and handsome, his hands, firmly planted beneath him as he held himself up. If she mated with this man, he would always take care of things, always support her, and never let anything happen to her. She could feel it in his strength and the way he insisted on control when they made love.

He wanted to do it all himself, and he was completely focused on her pleasure rather than his. It was foreign to her but it was wonderful, and she wanted to slow the feeling building inside her so she could enjoy it a little longer. But she could tell another orgasm was coming and she had no ability to resist it.

"Thor," she said.

"Princess," he answered, withdrawing and diving deep.

Her breaths were ragged, torn out of her, and she held on against the onslaught of sensation. "Please," she said, not knowing what she was asking for.

He reached between them and stroked gently over the spot that he'd tortured with his mouth before. It was too much sensation combined and she screamed as feeling overwhelmed her. Sheer emotional fire engulfed her as her body tensed up and then released into a waterfall of refreshing pleasure.

She closed her eyes against it and let her body give into the pleasure he was giving. Then she felt him jerk against her and opened her eyes because she wanted to see this. She wanted to see him go from the pleasure she was giving him.

His face tightened and his muscles bunched as he jerked against her. The feel of him inside her, going as she went, was incredible. She looked down between their bodies and couldn't tell where he began or she ended. It didn't matter, as long as it felt like this every time. As long as he made her forget there was anything in the world except for them.

As the pleasure abated, she scented the air. The smell of him, the smell of her, the smell of lovemaking, and the smell of the cabin, of wood logs and pine trees and mountain.

The smell of freedom and pleasure. Two things she'd never had before coming back to him. She let him rest against her and put her hands in his hair, stroking and feeling it as she'd always wanted to. They'd gone as far as they could go without mating. If the condom hadn't been there, they'd be permanently and irrevocably one another's, and the thought made her sort of wistful and sad.

If only things could be certain enough for that.

But no matter what, she had tonight.

He was already pulling out, grabbing a towel to clean off as she sat up slowly, watching him. Damn, that body was something. Tall and tanned and just delicious. And it had just been on top of her. He'd just been inside her. And nothing had ever felt more right in all the world.

"Thor?" she asked, twisting the sheets in her hands as she waited for him to join her in bed again. He tossed the towel in a hamper and turned to face her, proud and naked.

"Yes?" he asked.

I love you, she thought. But she couldn't say it. It wouldn't be fair. It wouldn't make sense. Maybe she was just being swept off her feet by the first wolf to pursue her. By his talk of red threads and fated mates. "Nothing," she said.

He grinned and jumped into bed with her. He wrapped his arms around her from behind and molded their bodies together, him the big spoon, she the small one. But she didn't mind being the smaller one when he was around. She knew he'd protect her.

Just like she'd protect him if it ever came to that.

"Lacey?" he asked quietly, his strong arms making her feel safe and warm and slightly sleepy.

"Yes?"

"I love you," he said.

She felt her body freeze against him. Suddenly it was too painful to stay there with him. She pushed away and sat up. Then she stood, looking for her clothing and a new set of wraps.

"Did I do something wrong?" he asked, hurt flashing in his eyes as he watched her. "Come back to bed."

"I can't," she said. "I can't do this anymore."

He just watched her, hurt and confusion mingling together in those honey colored eyes.

"I just, it's getting too confusing," she said. She knew it wasn't fair. That she'd just felt the same love for him and wanted to say it despite it being ridiculous. But hearing it, having it stated aloud, that was too much.

Being with him had been everything she'd dreamed of, but it couldn't just go on this way. They were from different worlds, and her world was bound to catch up with them eventually. She'd tried not to think about it. She'd wanted just a few moments with the man who felt she was the other end of his red thread. But hearing him say he loved her made it impossible to live in a dream.

"I'm still not ready to be your mate," she said. "I can't. Not until I know what the future holds."

He nodded. "Then just know I love you, no matter what happens. You're it for me, Lacey, or Matt, or whoever you are. You're my mate, my queen. And in the end, we'll be together. I know it."

Her heart clenched. She wished she could know the same thing. She wished she didn't get the sense that something dangerous was closing in. She wished she could tell him she loved him, too. But that would make everything so final, and she wasn't ready for that.

She wasn't ready to be loved. Not until she knew she was out of danger. So she stood there staring at him, not knowing what to say to his declaration. Not knowing what to do about the situation.

And then her phone beeped. Her heart jumped and she rummaged in her bag. She'd gotten a new phone before leaving, and only one person had the number. One person she was close to, who knew she was leaving and was always on her side.

One person who promised not to contact her unless it was completely urgent. Her cousin, Fifi.

She flipped open the phone to find a text from him telling her to call him when she got a second.

Damn, she didn't want to leave things like this with Thor, but she knew Fifi didn't play around, and would only bother her if it was an emergency. She sent Thor a pleading expression, begging him to understand.

"Go," he said, waving a hand.

Her heart thudded painfully but she nodded. They'd have to work out whatever was between them when she got back.

***

She walked out of the cabin and into the night air. It was dark and crisp and the mountains smelled different at night. All her senses were on alert to make sure no one was out here. When she didn't sense or scent anyone, she lifted the phone to her ear and hit the call button.

Fifi picked up on the first ring. His deep voice was reassuring and alarming at the same time. "Hi, girl," he said. "How's it going?"

She glanced around her once again with a hand over the speaker. Then she answered. "It's going okay."

"They've found you," he said. One simple word, but it meant so much. It meant the fairytale of the last few days was over. It meant she was right to walk away from Thor when he said he loved her. Maybe her gut had known something she hadn't.

"I know," she said. "I had a feeling."

He exhaled against the speaker and the phone cracked. "I'm sorry hon."

She sighed. "It's okay. So what happens now?"

"I don't know," he said. "I can't tell you to come back because they still plan to marry you off. Make you disappear. If they know what they mean to do next, they haven't told me."

"Oh," she said.

"But they aren't going to do something that draws a lot of attention," he said. "So it's best to probably just wait it out and call their bluff. They don't want your new pack seeing it and then word getting out that they can't control their own family."

"Right," she said. "The reputation of the pack is everything."

"Right," he said. "So I guess the only answer is me coming out there to protect you."

"No," she said, leaning against the side of the house and keeping her voice low. "You can't. You can't put yourself at risk like that."

"Lacey, I'm one of their assassins. If they've sent someone after you, I'm the one who can take them on."

"I can't ask you to."

"You've never needed to," he said softly. "You're the only one who has ever understood me. My best friend. I'm not letting them do this. If someone is coming for you, I'm going to be there."

Her eyes watered. Fifi, real name Felix, had been one of the only people who knew who she was. And she'd known who he was. When others had seen a boy, he'd known she was a girl controlled by her father. When others had seen a feminine, tall, ridiculously beautiful man, she'd seen a man who lived to carry out missions that no one else could handle.

Because Fifi had a unique alpha power: the ability to put people (and shifters) to sleep.

Her family was full of unique alpha powers. They'd been bred from pure alphas for centuries and some of the most powerful gifts could only be found in their line.

But she knew what the tribunal had on Fifi, and she couldn't let him risk it. "I can't have you come out here, Felix," she said.

"Uh oh," he replied. "Using my full name. You're serious."

"Yes," she said. "I want you to stay away. Stay safe." She was one of the few people who took Fifi seriously and understood the man behind the mask. He had enough problems without running after her.

Years ago, when she'd gone to that mansion to watch Thor and the others compete in that alpha challenge, Fifi had come to watch over her, to be a bodyguard and protect her secrets. Misty had found her out, coming in when she was changing, and they'd made a sort of friendship right then. One of her only girl friends, though she hadn't really kept in touch over the years.

Fifi had been with her then. Had been with her for many missions. But she wasn't Matt anymore. She wasn't important to the tribunal anymore. It wasn't safe for Fifi to guard her anymore.

"So you really don't want me to come," he said quietly.

"No," she said.

"Too bad," a voice called out in the night. She glanced up, realizing the noise had come from the woods in front of her and not from her phone. "Because I'm already here."

CHAPTER 14

He was tall, unbelievably tall even for a shifter, with long, pale hair bound in a loose ponytail and ephemeral features that nearly glittered in the moonlight. His body was lean and strong, but she knew how deadly it could be. But his grin… His grin was all Fifi. Devastating and sardonic and strong all at once. He strode toward her lazily, hands in the pockets of that white linen suit he liked to wear, and she was all at once incredibly mad at him for coming and intensely relieved to see him.

It was a little like coming home.

She ran to him across the grass, throwing out her arms to grasp him in a tight bear hug. He reached down and lifted her up and hugged her to him for a moment. Then he released her and wrinkled his nose.

"You smell," he said, tilting his head to the side. "Like wolf." He looked up at the cabin ahead of him. "Who are you staying with? I only knew you'd sought out an alpha. Someone who owed you a favor. I had a guess…" The cabin door banged as someone opened it too quickly and she heard footsteps pounding behind her. A low growl in the distance.

She turned to see Thor striding from the house, looking angry at the fact that Fifi was holding her. "Shit," she said, looking at Fifi helplessly. Fifi simply set her aside and rolled up his sleeves.

"Don't hurt him," she said.

Fifi raised a blond eyebrow. "Getting feelings for the mutt, are you? I always knew something was weird about you two. You fought too much at the mansion."

She flushed. "I know. Everyone has already pointed that out. What are you going to do?" She turned to stand next to him as Thor stalked toward them. When he jumped into wolf form and ran forward, she put a hand over her face. She could try to call him off but she had a feeling it would be fruitless.

"Thor…" she said.

Thor sent her a glance but then focused back on his prey: Fifi.

Fifi leaped elegantly forward into his wolf, leaving his clothes behind on the grass, and the two wolves met in the center of the clearing, tussling under the moonlight. She ran forward, not knowing if she had the energy to discharge her alpha power again.

"Stop!" she called out. "All of you, stop!"

But they kept tussling. Fifi was having a more difficult time than she would have expected. Normally he'd have the other wolf firmly by the scruff of his neck, but Thor was putting up a better fight than she would have thought, given that he wasn't a trained assassin.

He was pure alpha, and it showed in the strength and speed of his movements. When it looked like he was bout to get the upper hand, Fifi sent her an exasperated look and she nodded, giving him permission to put Thor to sleep.

The scent of lavender filled the clearing, a pleasant but menacing smell slightly tinged with musk and woods. Thor sent her an alarmed glance and let out a low growl as he fought the urge to sleep, but then the huge wolf went silent and fell to the ground beneath Fifi.

Fifi used a paw to turn him over and check his pulse. Her heart caught in her throat and when he nodded that Thor was fine, she felt like she could finally breathe again. Why did she already have to care about him so much? She strode forward to where Fifi was transforming and putting his clothes back on. He draped his jacket over Thor's transforming body, but not before taking a good look at it. Fifi liked males and females, and Thor was an amazing specimen.

She growled as she ran for Thor's pants and told Fifi to look away as she put them on.

A low growl sounded, making the hairs on the back of her neck stand up in anticipation as a low, furious voice spoke.

Fifi tossed his hair over his shoulder and looked up at the figure approaching out of the darkness. Lock was tall. Not as tall as Fifi, but with the anger emanating from him at this moment, she wouldn't bet against him in a fight.

"What did you do to my brother?" he asked, flashing a fang and shedding his leather jacket. Beneath it he wore a worn tee shirt with a skull on the front in black.

Fifi grinned. "Lock, nice to see you again. Last time I believe it was...oh yes, I was saving your butt."

Lock's expression just darkened and his eyes lit on Matt's hands on Thor. "Get your hands off him. I knew you were a betrayer. I knew you were—"

Fifi was there at the next second, holding an arm around Lock's neck as Lock growled in frustration.

"Be careful what you say to my cousin. It's thanks to her I didn't kill your dumbass brother for attacking me over nothing," Fifi said, stroking a long finger against Lock's face.

Lock's amber eyes flashed in the darkness and he turned to look at Fifi. "Your cousin? I knew you two were related, but I had no idea..."

"What you don't know could fill a book," Fifi said, keeping his arm around Lock's neck. "So maybe just shut up and let Lacey explain."

"Lacey?" Lock asked, looking her up and down curiously.

"Her real name," Fifi hissed, letting the other alpha go.

Lock brushed himself off and picked up his jacket as he walked over to Thor. He knelt beside his brother to take his pulse and then breathed out a sigh of relief when he found he was fine. When Lock turned to Matt she saw sweat sheening his forehead and worry lines beneath his eyes. Lock truly cared for his brother.

"I wouldn't let anyone hurt Thor," she said.

Lock was silent for a moment, ran a hand through Thor's tousled hair, and then pinned an accusing glance on her. "You mean, no one except you?" he asked.

"No. What do you mean?" she responded.

Lock looked down at his brother again. "You mean, you actually plan to leave the tribunal behind and live out here in the middle of nowhere with my brother?"

"The tribunal is no home for me, now," she said, coming forward so she could touch Thor as well, ignoring Lock's possessive growl. "And it's beautiful out here. But if I do leave, it will be to *avoid* hurting him. Not to hurt him."

Lock's expression changed slightly and he frowned. "I've been fucking everything up since I came back here, haven't I?"

"Yes," Fifi said sardonically.

Matt laughed, nodding. "But that's okay. Thor's pretty good at it as well."

"What do you mean?" Lock asked, standing and lifting Thor in his arms like he weighed nothing.

"I mean, he's used to putting his foot in it a lot as well, so I bet he'll be quick to forgive you."

Lock paused halfway to the cabin. "And you? Will you be quick to forgive me?"

Fifi snorted. "If she is I won't be. Someone's got to keep an eye on your ass."

"And you'd be more than happy to do that, wouldn't you?" Lock mumbled.

Fifi just laughed and followed them back to the cabin. When they got there, Fifi held the door open and Lock walked in and deposited Thor on a couch. He looked so peaceful while sleeping. It wasn't until they were all seated and quiet and the door to the outside was shut that Lock suddenly narrowed his eyes and looked between them, scenting the air.

"You two had sex, didn't you?"

She flushed deeply. Damn being a wolf and having absolutely no privacy. Any animal in the vicinity would be aware of what had happened. But she had to remind herself that there was nothing to be ashamed of.

"We were just testing our compatibility," she said. Taking a taste is more like it, she admitted to herself. "After all, we are considering each other as mates."

"An odd pairing if I ever saw one," Fifi muttered.

"Damn straight," Lock said. "Wait." He sat up straighter in his chair. "What do you mean? We have full alpha blood, nearly as pure as yours, I'd wager. Though I'm guessing you know that."

Fifi stayed silent and Matt looked at him curiously. "What is it?" she asked.

Fifi frowned. "I don't know, Matt. There are things you shouldn't know about the tribunal. Things you can't go back on knowing, things you can't do anything about even if you do know."

"I want to know," she said.

"Yeah," Lock said. "She wants to know."

Fifi sighed. "First, I want you to know I was never a part of this. I just know it happened, because with my training it's not hard to put together. Secondly, the tribunal hasn't done this with any other generation. It happened because of your father."

"What?" she asked. "What happened?" Her stomach twisted with dread and she glanced at Thor, hoping whatever Fifi told her wasn't going to make everything between them impossible.

"When your father was growing up, there was a squad," he said.

"What kind of squad?"

"They made sure that several threats were eliminated."

"What do you mean threats?" Lock asked. "My parents were innocent of anything but being strong enough to attract your notice. And what about Misty's parents? I thought you were friends—"

Fifi put up a hand to silence them. "Some of this I've only learned in the last few years. For instance, after you were captured and I heard them speaking cryptically about your bloodline. Anyway, if you think your parents were totally innocent, then you only got half of the story."

"What do you mean?" Lacey asked, wrapping a hand around her waist as if it could soothe away the nervousness coiling inside her with every word.

"Several clans were planning to overthrow the tribunal," Fifi said. "By force, if necessary. They'd found out that a plague that affected females in particular had been released by the tribunal on accident. But the cure wasn't released with it. Now, I'm not saying it wasn't evil, what they did by not addressing it and saving wolves. I'm not saying their motives were pure, as I'm sure they didn't fail to notice the benefit to them if other packs lost alphas. But the original plague wasn't meant for wolves at all. It was meant for humans. It was meant to easily kill those who sought out our kind and wouldn't relent."

Matt's mouth gaped open. She'd thought she'd been privy to so much of the tribunal's inner workings, and she had, regarding the present. But she'd been naive about the past. About the murmurings and the rumors she'd heard.

"So they killed my parents to shut them up, because my mother was a scientist at the lab that leaked the virus. She knew what had happened," Lock said.

"No, they killed your parents because they were afraid that all of wolf society would be lost in a war with itself. It seemed like the lesser sacrifice. Misty's father worked in the same lab, and he was aware as well. That's why your parents were working together."

"How come you never told me this?" Lacey asked, blinking away tears of anger at her family.

"I didn't see any point," Fifi said. "You were their puppet, and you were happy, at least as much as you could be, until they turned on you. And then there was no time. And what's done is done. What is the point of rehashing it?"

"Justice is the point of rehashing it!" Lock said, and Lacey had to agree.

She nodded. "They can't get away with it."

"They're going to have to," Thor said, sitting up groggily and rubbing his head. He glanced around until his amber eyes rested on Matt, and then he calmed. "Because I'm not letting you go back there. Any of you."

"Oh?" Fifi asked. "And you'd stop me?"

"If you were going to tell them where she was, yes."

"No," Fifi said, shaking his head and folding his arms. "When I go back to that glass prison, I won't take her with me. It's mine and mine alone."

Lacey's heart ached for him. For the fact that he knew just how evil the tribunal was but couldn't do anything about it. He had to stay, he had no choice. But he'd come here for her, to defend her if needed, knowing that for him, he'd have to go back there at some point. He wouldn't have a choice.

She gritted her teeth. The whole thing was so fucked up. Had become so dark.

"So, what do we do now?" she asked, turning to Thor, who put an arm around her possessively and glowered at the rest of them.

"I don't know," he said darkly. "All I know is that none of you are taking her from my side."

Fifi tilted his head to the side pensively. "Well, if you want to keep her, that attitude is exactly what you are going to need to do it."

"And stop trying to attack my cousin," she said.

"Sorry," Thor muttered, stroking her hair. "But when I see a male touching my female, I don't care who he is. My wolf wants his blood."

"Well tell your wolf I'm not his female yet, and I won't be if he doesn't calm down."

That shut him up.

CHAPTER 15

While Lock talked to Fifi, Thor guided Matt over to a hall where they could be alone. Then he pressed her up against a wall, hands planted on either side of her head.

She didn't feel intimidated. She knew him too well by now to be afraid that he would hurt her. But she did find herself afraid of the deep longing in his eyes. The possessive intensity there.

"Remember that time we were playing football at the mansion and you tackled me?" she asked, reaching up to stroke his hair. He shook away from her hand with a snort and pinned a firm gaze on her again.

"I was a douche, I know. But I thought you were a dude, like everyone else did."

"I know," she said. "It's just funny thinking of moments like that."

"I need to know you won't leave me," he said, stroking her hair back and looking down her body as if to make sure she was okay.

"Leave you?"

"You picked up the phone and you were gone. And when you didn't come back in right away, I didn't know what to do. I wanted to give you space to come to terms with things. I know it feels like I'm rushing you, but I can't help it. Not many people know you yet. When they do, things will get more complicated."

"So you want to claim an alpha female before others know about it?" she asked, vaguely offended. He put a hand in his hair and pushed off the wall to pace back and forth in front of her.

"If you think that's all it is, you don't know me at all," he said. "I have feelings for you. You know that. I think you're my fated mate. I think you're my red thread. I don't care that it's going fast. I just want to mate you soon so you can't run away, thinking it's for my own good."

She swallowed. She understood what he meant. Once they were mated, leaving him would never be the right thing. They would be only with each other for life. Leaving him would be cruel, dooming him to be alone.

Thus she wasn't ready to mate him yet.

"I don't know," she said. "For me, it's almost been enough just being here. Loving you, knowing there's someone I could have loved, in a different life."

He frowned and pinned her with a glare again. So tall, so upset. "And why not this one?"

She swiped at a tear that threatened her eye. "Fifi called because they've found me. They know where I am."

"Oh," Thor said gravely.

"He doesn't think they would do something drastic and make things overtly public in front of your family, but at the same time, he doesn't think I should go back there. But thinking about it, the only thing I can think of now, is that Fifi and I should move on."

"Why not stay here?" Thor asked, keeping his hands on either side of her head, pinning her there. She could still hear the others in the next room, arguing quietly about what they knew.

"Fifi told me about the tribunal. How much did Lock tell you?"

"Everything," he said. "That your parents arranged to have mine killed."

"Did he tell you it was because your parents and a few others were planning to uproot the tribunal?"

"No," he said, his brow crumpling in confusion. "What do you mean?"

"Apparently they were upset about some plague leak or something, and they wanted to expose it to the rest of the shifter world. But it was all an accident."

Thor let out a deep sigh. "Why doesn't anyone get that this doesn't matter to me?" He held out his hands for her to see. "All I want is to protect what I can with these two hands. All I want to do is see my pack mates, my family, and my mate safe." He shook his head. "That's all I can do. I can't go back and change the past. I can't overthrow our ruling system. Maybe Lock could, if he rallied enough wolves around him. But that's not for me. I just want to make those around me happy. I just want to forget and move on. Can you do that with me?"

She touched his face. "I loved what we shared before. Maybe I even love you. But as long as I'm with you, that simple future you crave just isn't possible. They will come for me eventually."

He shook his head vehemently. "I won't let them."

"You won't have a choice." She cupped his chin but he avoided her eyes. "Thor, what would stop them from doing something like they did last time, and hiring someone to off me because I'm a problem, like they hired someone to off your parents?"

"I'm here, that's what," he grumbled. "You don't get it. I would die for you. If you leave here, it's meaningless for me."

"You have your pack, you have to think of that. I'll be safe. Fifi is one of their assassins…"

"That explains why he beat me," he said. "Did he actually put me to sleep? I didn't even know that was an alpha power."

She nodded hesitantly.

"Your family has some crazy abilities," he said.

She nodded again.

"But mine does too. I do too. And your family doesn't even know about them. So why don't you believe me when I say you can trust me?"

"I'm safer with Fifi," she said. "After all, he beat you, didn't he?"

"I would be ready for him this time. And what are the chances another wolf has that gift?"

"How can you be ready for that? What exactly are your alpha powers anyway?" she asked.

He shook his head. "I'm not telling you. Not until you agree to mate me. Not until you trust me."

"That's going to be a while then," she said. "Because I'm not going to walk into your life and ruin your dreams and everything you've worked for. Not for a little sex."

"Is that what this is to you? A little sex?" he snarled. "Don't lie. We both know it's so much more."

She turned away. If it was, she wouldn't admit it. There was no point getting her heart broken over this. She had a few days of safety and freedom with him to remember. But when shit hit the fan and the tribunal made their move, there was no telling what would happen.

But she'd never wished harder that her life was her own. That she was one of her sisters rather than the one chosen to be raised as a boy.

More like a slave.

She blinked away tears and tried to hide them from Thor. There was no point crying at a time like this. Besides, she never cried. She'd been numb for a long time, pushing her true self down below the surface.

So why couldn't she do that now, so she could walk away from him cleanly? He was asking her to stay, and she found herself wanting to.

"You won't give me any promises?" he asked quietly, tilting her chin to look into her eyes.

She nodded.

He sighed in resignation and took her hand. "At least stay with me tonight?" he asked. "Let me know you're safe one more night? And then you and Fifi can make plans in the morning."

She nodded. She was too tired to travel tonight anyway. Everything had happened so fast. With the wolf fight and Lock appearing, she hadn't had much time to adjust to the news Fifi had told her on the phone. Or him appearing to guard her.

Everything would change tomorrow. But tonight, she would sleep in his arms as if she'd never left him after they'd made love. It would be the last good day. The last one they had for sure. She let him take her hand and lead her to his bedroom. Let him hold up the covers while she got in. Let him go out and tell the others they were going to bed and weather their teasing.

Then she let him come back in, turn off the lights, and curl around her, giving her warmth and holding her like she was the only thing that mattered to him.

The rest of the world could wait.

CHAPTER 16

She woke to a loud knock on the door. Thor was still quietly snoring, so she lifted his heavily muscled arm so that she could sit up and look around. It was early morning and sunlight was just beginning to stream through the drapes. She tried to gently get out of bed but Thor's hand shot out and caught her shirt.

"Where are you going?" he asked.

"Someone knocked," she said, gesturing to the door.

He groaned and sat up, rubbing his eyes. "I swear, every day is an adventure with you." Then he looked at the door again, this time with a new look in his eyes. "Oh wait, Fifi is here."

"His real name is Felix, you know," she said, smiling slightly. "Just so you know that he has an actual name that isn't ridiculous."

"I don't mind the name Fifi," he said. "It suits him. Kind of like Matt suits you."

"How does Matt suit me?" she asked, folding her arms and waiting for an explanation.

"Um, you're…I don't know. It just does." He rolled out of bed and grabbed a robe from the edge of a chair, putting it on as he went to the door. She loved the sight of his wide back and muscled legs.

Thor opened the door and someone spoke to him in a low voice. He responded and she cleared her throat, keeping the covers drawn up over her as she tried to see who was at the door. It was Lock.

He gave her a long, slow once over and then winked. Thor let out a growl. "Easy, bro," Lock said. "Calm down, she's yours."

"Not yet I'm not," she said.

Lock raised an eyebrow and then turned back to Thor. "There's news. Fifi got a call early this morning. From someone in the tribunal, asking him to meet with them."

She jumped out of bed, reaching for her jacket and sliding her arms into it and zipping it up as she joined them at the door. "What do you mean?"

"He went out early this morning and hasn't been back," he said. When she turned to him with wide eyes, he put up a hand. "Fifi told me not to bother you. He said he could handle it himself. And frankly, I didn't need you and Thor walking into a trap with him if that was what was happening."

"He knew they were on to me, but I don't think he knew they would be out here this fast. Maybe they followed him." She tried to push past them. "I need to go find him. I don't want him in trouble because of me."

Thor grabbed her arm, stopping her. "I don't want you in trouble because of him."

"They can't hurt me as much as they can hurt him," she said. "He never should have come. I'm the one who ran away. I had nothing to lose. He had everything."

"What do you mean?" Thor asked, holding her by the shoulders. "What do they have on him?"

She shook her head. "I can't say, but I have to go to him. He can't be out there alone. How long as he been gone?"

Lock looked at his phone. "About five minutes longer than he said he'd be gone. That's why I knocked."

She put a hand on his shoulder. "You did the right thing. I'm going to go get my breast wraps on. Then we'll head out."

"We will do no such thing," Thor said angrily. "Lock and I will head out to save your cousin, and you will stay here."

"You might need my powers," she said.

Thor and Lock looked at each other and smirked.

"No," Thor said. "I think we'll be fine. Between the two of us we can take nearly anyone. Trust me, Matt. You haven't even seen the beginning of what I can do yet. I fought Fifi the other night fairly, carefully, because I knew he meant something to you. But if you or someone you care about is in danger, I can be a whole different wolf."

"That he can," Lock said, flashing a fang. "And I can back him up."

She sighed. "I'd feel better if you could tell me what you can do."

"No," Thor said. "Trust me or don't. But you are staying here."

"I could use my alpha power on you," she said. "Stop you from going."

"But that would stop you from going as well," Thor said. "And who would save Fifi?"

She growled. "He might not need any saving. Honestly, all they want is me. If you let me go out there, all of you, including Fifi, can avoid being hurt. He is my father. It's time to talk to him."

Thor shook his head. "No. We will talk to him. Or whoever he has sent. But I need you here. I need to know you are safe."

"You're not being reasonable," she said, feeling her throat tense. "Lock, tell him."

Lock sighed and folded his arms. "I can't. He's decided you're his mate. As his brother, I'm here to back him up and protect you." He and Thor walked to the door together and he turned back at the last minute. "Welcome to the pack."

"You can't just go out and fight for me. I haven't even agreed to mate you," she said, exasperated that these males were going to override her wishes. Sure, they had more brute strength, and sure, it was for her own good. But she was allowed to be protective too, and now everyone she cared about would be out there at once, with men she knew to be ruthless.

"We're going," Thor said. "Promise me you'll stay inside."

She sighed. "Fine." There was no going around it. Hopefully whomever the tribunal sent wouldn't harm Fifi. Maybe he could even negotiate. Reassure them that she was no threat. Tell them that letting her stay here with Thor, mated, wasn't a bad idea.

Mated. Weeks ago she couldn't have imagined it. Now she didn't know how to live if it didn't happen. She paced inside the cabin until Thor and his brother left, and then watched them change into wolves and scent the air before darting off together into the grass.

She locked the door behind them and went to her room to change. She pulled a fresh pair of breast wraps out and sighed heavily as she started to put them on. Being free for a while had been liberating, and they really were uncomfortable.

A knock sounded at the door. "Thor?" Was he back already? She tied her wraps hastily and threw her tee shirt over her head and was halfway into her jacket when the front door burst open.

She stopped dead when she saw who was there. Not Thor, Lock or Fifi.

It was Ernie, Thor's second in command.

His gray hair was mussed, and his young face was harried. "Are you alone?" he asked.

A tingle went down her spine. He was Thor's second, but he was still an alpha male. Maybe she should lie.

154

He scented the air. Too late. "You are."

She didn't like the gleam in his eyes so she took a step back from the entryway, folding her arms and trying to look calm while she tried to think which direction would be the best to run away. Should she bolt past him out the door? Should she jump through a window? Lock herself in Thor's bedroom? She didn't know his alpha powers, so it was possible he had super strength, like Lindon's family had.

He watched her like a snake eyeing a mouse. What was his angle?

She looked to the window, but Thor and Lock were no longer in sight. Her heart pounded. She'd have to get out of this herself. Ironic that Thor had made her promise to stay here and be safe, but she wouldn't be safe if she stayed.

"What do you want?" she asked. "Thor's not here."

He nodded. "I know."

Her heart sank. Was he a part of all of this? Connected with the tribunal? He hadn't been around since the first time she'd seen him, so she'd forgotten to ask Thor more about him.

He walked forward, something in his hands, and she looked down to see he was holding a rope.

"What's that for?" she asked.

"To make sure you come with me. Your father sent me," he said.

"My father?"

He nodded. "You know, the one who killed Thor's parents and left my father to run the pack here. My father, whom Thor threw out. Not that I like my father, I don't. But I also know that you don't want to cross the tribunal. So I got in touch with them to let them know there was an alpha on the loose."

She took another step back, trying to buy time. "Traitor. You betrayed your alpha."

"He put the whole pack in danger," he said.

"But that's not why you're doing this," she said, moving back again.

He took a step forward, coiling the rope slowly. "You're right. I don't want to live here as beta all my life. When I deliver you to the tribunal and solve their problems, they're going to solve some of mine. I'll finally have the life I deserve."

"What did they promise you?" she asked.

"Whatever I wanted. Money. Advantaged access to an alpha female." He looked her over. "Though, now that I think about it, maybe I would be better off just taking you. If I mated you, their problem would be solved anyway and I'd be mated to one of the most powerful females in the species."

She swallowed. Hell no. Hell no would she mate with this man and let him hide her from the world like her father wanted for the rest of her life. Hell no would she be his ticket to happiness while he was her ticket to misery.

She got into a light boxing stance with one foot behind the other, ready to fight him if she needed to.

He waggled a finger. "Not so fast. I saw how you fight. I didn't want to deal with it." He pulled something from his pocket, lifted it to his mouth, and she didn't have time to dodge before it launched right into her abdomen with a sharp pain. She hissed and looked down to see a small dart. She pulled it out as dizziness waved through her.

"What have you done to me?" she asked, as the room started to wave in front of her. An incredible sense of vertigo came over her and she fell forward, catching herself on her hands and knees. She could hear her own heartbeat, pounding in her ears, as she looked blearily around, waiting for the world to stop spinning.

He walked over to her, easily able to catch her now that she was incapacitated and getting worse by the minute. She struggled but he pulled her hands up and together and started to bind them. "I just made it easier on both of us, princess," he said. "I just made it easier on both of us."

Her last sound was a growl as he lifted her onto his shoulder, and then she went unconscious.

CHAPTER 17

Thor followed Fifi's scent out across the wet morning grass. It felt good to have Lock beside him, backing him up for the first time in so long. His twin was a part of him, and things felt more complete when he was around. But soon he would take a mate, and things would never be the same.

But first, he needed to find her cousin. He couldn't smell the scent of a wolf in distress, so he wasn't sure if they just hadn't found Fifi, or if Fifi was simply calm because he was highly trained. Who would have thought the pretty, aggravating man was so capable? But Thor could be capable too.

His blood burned with the need to protect his mate, and whatever his mate wanted to protect.

"You smell that?" Lock asked, veering to change direction. Thor did. He followed Lock toward the unfamiliar scent that was becoming stronger as they dodged through the trees and underbrush toward the road at the base of the mountain. They kept running until headlights came into view at the entrance to the woods. They were a good distance from the cabin now, and he tried not to be nervous about Matt being back there alone.

There was no one to threaten her, after all. Everyone should be out here.

But still, they needed to get this over with quickly. He put a paw up for Lock to wait, and crept slowly to a nearby tree so they could see what was going on.

Fifi was there, his bright blonde hair glowing white in the sunlight.

And a man, a shorter, portly man in a gray pin striped suit was pacing in front of him.

Fifi's shirt was torn and Thor couldn't see his face because his hair was free of his ponytail and hanging loose, obscuring his expression. But from the way the portly man paced, he could tell something was off. He looked down to Fifi's hands and saw they were tied.

Anger raged through him. He was naturally protective of anything that was his. Matt was his, and Fifi was someone Matt loved, so he would be someone Thor loved.

The alpha in him howled to attack, but he made himself wait.

Fifi raised his head to speak. "You won't find her. She's not here. I told her to run already."

"We'll see," the man said. "I have someone on it."

Fifi seemed shocked. "What?"

"Someone called in to report a suspicious person. Interestingly enough, they picked up on the fact that she was female."

Thor's stomach clenched and he shared a worried look with Lock. Who could it be?

It hit him instantly and made him want to turn tail and run for the cabin.

Ernie.

"I think it's the beta of the small pack here. Ernest, or something?" the man said, pacing in front of Fifi. He checked his watch. "But he was supposed to be back here right now. Maybe I should go check…"

Fifi's head whipped up in alarm. "What do you mean?"

"He was supposed to bring her back here. He said he had a key to the cabin, so it would have been easy to get in."

Fifi whipped his head toward the woods, looking right at Thor for a split second. What was he trying to tell him?

"Maybe he's getting ideas. He's only supposed to bring her here so we can talk and take her back to her father. He's not supposed to take anything into his own hands."

Fifi moved and Thor could see him fiddling with his hands. Maybe to try and untie himself? Thor itched to run for the cabin, but he knew Matt could defend herself against the likes of Ernie. She'd done it before. And if someone showed up, he knew she'd scream, and he wasn't so far away that he couldn't hear it.

Still, his heart went cold with fear at the thought of someone going after her, and he itched to run back and check.

"So, you had someone go pick her up, when you knew she'd be vulnerable because her alphas were out here finding me, and then you sent an unmated alpha male in that you didn't know to find her?" Fifi asked, exasperated.

"Now that you mention it, it does sound a little careless. But forgiving me for thinking that someone who thinks enough of the Tribunal to tip us off wouldn't then go and piss us off." The man pulled sunglasses out of his pocket and put them on to look out toward the cabin.

Thor stifled a growl at the look of the man's face. Hard, craggy. Someone he didn't want within three feet of Matt.

But he was concerned that whomever was supposed to bring Matt here wasn't here. He wanted to turn and run to find her, but didn't know if it was better to wait and engage whomever he had to fight all at once here.

"Thor?" Lock said quietly.

"Yes?"

"I'm worried about Matt. I'll take care of Fifi, you go get your girl."

"They might have weapons," Thor replied. "It could be dangerous."

"I know," Lock said. "But you're right. What's important right now isn't the past, it's the future. And that girl is your future. And another alpha could be claiming her right now."

Panicked surged through Thor. "What do you mean?"

"Well, if he hasn't showed up, doesn't that mean maybe he's decided to just keep her for himself? After all, if he mates her, he has some serious bargaining power."

Rage surged through Thor and he scented the air. His hearing was keen. If she had been taken, surely he would know. But yet…

"Shit," he said. "I have to go back and check. I don't want to leave you here, but I just… I have to."

"Go," Lock said. "Fifi and I will figure it out. He knows we're here. I could see it in his eyes when he looked over."

Thor nodded. She should be fine. But he had to go see for himself.

He turned and ran back through the woods in the direction of the cabin, listening for any sound from his mate. Any scent of his mate.

And then, on the wind, as he ran as fast as his legs could carry him back the way he came, he heard it.

A faint scream, carried toward him on the wind.

Behind him, he heard chaos break out at the car. Lock must have made his move.

But he'd have to trust Lock and Fifi to take care of things on their own. His mate was in danger.

***

Matt woke up tired and extremely angry. Ernie was bending over her, looking like he'd just been standing there watching her. She looked around, not recognizing their surroundings.

"Where are we?" she asked groggily. She tried to move and the world spun rapidly. "Damn it."

"Language," Ernie said quietly. "If you're going to be my mate, I'd prefer you to be a little more gentle-mannered." She growled at him and he grabbed her by the back of her head and jerked her to face him.

"I'm never going to mate you," she said.

He looked over her body, which was luckily still dressed and wrapped. "We'll see. You know, I knew you were a female from the minute I met you."

"You seemed to believe Thor once he insisted."

Ernie shrugged. "Not for long. That's why when I called the tribunal I told them there was an alpha female on the run. Not a male. They confirmed it. Didn't even try not to. I think they'd assumed you'd gone rogue as a female to hide your identity. You know, I almost want to see what they could do for me if I brought you back. But then again, going back as your mate gives me even more bargaining power."

She shook her head. "That won't stop them from killing you if they want to."

Ernie hesitated, but then his eyes lit on her chest. "Maybe I should see what I'm risking it for then."

She swallowed. Her hands were bound behind her back, so she'd be helpless to stop him if he tried something. But no one but Thor had seen her breasts, and she intended to keep it that way. She focused, getting ready to shift if needed to use her power. She was already incapacitated, so it wouldn't matter, as long as she negated him.

He reached for the bottom of her tee shirt and she relaxed, acting as if she didn't mean to stop him.

"Submissive," he said. "Good, I like that."

Bile rose in her throat but she made herself stay still as possible as he lifted her shirt to look at her wraps. She'd show him submissive in a second.

She'd make *him* submit to *her*.

Just as soon as she could shift.

He reached for the wraps, grazing the skin of her stomach, and she knew this was it. Time to move. She focused and calmed herself, thinking of her wolf and all of the things her wolf loved. But nothing happened.

She felt numb, weak, and the world spun once again. Not as badly as before, but still enough to make her want to retch. Either way, she leaned away from Ernie and gagged over the grass, hoping to be as unsexy as possible.

"Damn it," he said, grabbing the back of her shirt and pulling her up to face him again. "You tried to shift, didn't you? Well luckily my contact at the tribunal knew about your power and gave me these little darts that nullify your ability to shift." He looked at his watch. "It should be wearing off soon, so I guess if I want to mate you, I should do it as soon as possible."

"Rape is against our laws," she choked out, unable to believe this was happening, that she was this powerless. And she couldn't scent Thor. He'd left her completely unprotected, ironically while insisting on protecting her.

"Well, so is murder, but the tribunal committed that, didn't they?" He shook his head. "And why not? We are animals, the fittest survive. We get what we want at the cost of others. We act on instinct." He turned her head to the side and licked up her neck, and she let out a loud scream of anger, both to hopefully blow out his eardrums and draw the attention of anyone in the area.

She'd planned to take care of this herself, and she would have been able to without the drugs. So it was unfair that she now had to call Thor back from helping Fifi. But she needed to, and she would. She screamed again but he put a hand over her mouth.

She bit down hard and he growled and wrestled her back onto the ground, her bound arms painfully beneath her. She tried to kick out at him, but he moved out of the way, and she couldn't adjust quickly enough due to feeling disoriented.

He got between her legs and reached for the hem of her shirt again. She took a deep breath and focused for a moment, reminding herself who she was.

He wasn't the first wolf to try to hurt her. To try and force her to do something she didn't want. He had an advantage, but she was far from done fighting. She feigned being calm, and when he started to crawl over her, she brought her leg up hard between his, crushing him right in his alpha jewels.

She grinned as he howled and held himself and fell backwards. She pushed herself to her feet, fighting off waves of nausea and started to run, hoping she'd be able to shift soon, that her metabolism was faster than he'd planned.

But he caught her by the leg and jerked her down. Damn, how did he recover so fast?

"All right, that's it. This time you pay."

An angry snarl sounded before he could get on her again, and a giant red wolf went soaring over them to land on the other side of Ernie, growling dangerously.

"Get the fuck away from my mate," Thor said angrily. "Before I tear you to shreds."

She sighed in relief. He didn't need a snappy comeback. He just needed to be here. She slumped back wearily, willing her body to shift so she could help.

CHAPTER 18

Ernie turned to face Thor, who stood there, bristling angrily, reddish-brown fur glistening in the late morning light.

Matt moved her head side to side, trying to see if the world was still spinning. Only slightly. Only if she moved quickly.

"Be careful, Thor," she mumbled, trying to make the words as clear as possible even though her thoughts were thick as mud. "He's got weapons from the tribunal. Darts that make it so you can't shift."

Thor nodded at her, taking a second to look her up and down, making sure she was okay. She was now that he was here. She knew instinctively that nothing could happen to her when he was around. He was one of the most protective wolves she knew. Maybe the most.

"Threatening my female?" Thor asked. "I'm your alpha. How dare you?" He stepped forward and Ernie whimpered and stepped back, looking around him as if for an escape route.

"You never appreciated me," Ernie said. "You left this pack and only came back when you had your parents money to fix us all. But I was here the whole time. I saw what my father wrought. I saw the wreckage. And then you assumed that when you came back you would subjugate me."

"You could have challenged me for alpha," Thor said. "That would have been within our rules."

"But I'm not full alpha. Besides, I heard my uncle mention some of the alpha powers you have. I wasn't going to try that. Beta wasn't too bad, until I realized I'd never have a chance with a female."

"Many in our world won't have a chance with an alpha female."

"No," he said. "Any female. They all look to you, meanwhile you wait and wait for something that won't happen, an alpha female. And then you had one, and you thought she was a dude." Ernie snickered and Matt wondered why he didn't turn into his wolf form. Probably a good idea since Thor had already shifted.

"I knew she was a female, I just didn't want you touching her. But I never suspected you would go behind my back, like a snake, and steal her when I wasn't looking. When I thought she was protected. I trusted you."

"And that was a mistake," Ernie said, morphing into his wolf. "Let's finish this now."

"With pleasure," Thor said, crouching lightly. He was a predator, ready to fight, and he took her breath away.

She finally felt herself transform into her wolf. She breathed a sigh of relief and pushed her loosened bonds off her paws. Then she pushed up onto all four feet and tested her balance. Thor was distracted, looking over at her, and when Thor's attention was drawn, Ernie took his chance to run.

So much for finishing things now. Ernie took off across the grass, a gray bolt becoming smaller in the distance, and Thor started after him and then stopped, looking back at her. He let out a growl and she could see how hard it was for him not to go after the other wolf, but he restrained himself and walked back to her, licking her and making sure she was okay. She nuzzled against him, glad he had come and helped long enough for her to be herself again.

She leaned on him and he stood firm, being her strength. Her wolf was half as large as his, and she felt fully protected by him.

"You came," she said.

"Of course. No one touches my mate but me." He licked her again. "Are you okay? He didn't do anything?"

"No," she said. "I fought him."

"Good girl," he said. "I'm kind of disappointed I didn't get to tear him apart. When I saw him pull you down, I've never been more enraged in my life."

"And you get angry kind of easily."

"This is true," he said. "But you're fine and that's all that matters. I shouldn't have left you back there. I'm sorry."

"You thought the danger was all outside. I can't blame you."

"They have Fifi," he said. "I left Lock to try and help, but when I heard from the tribunal guy that someone was going to bring you to him, and that guy didn't show up, I had to run. I couldn't wait."

"It's fine," she said. "You came." She let out a little huff. "Normally I would have been able to take him. He had a dart gun and it knocked me out. And then he got weird ideas about mating, but I couldn't shift to use my alpha power on him."

Thor growled. "Damn it."

"If you hadn't come…"

"But I did," Thor replied. "And as soon as you accept me, I'm going to mate you once and for all so no other males can get any ideas about you belonging to anyone but me."

"What are we going to do about Fifi?" she asked.

"What are we going to do about anything?" he replied grimly. "The tribunal clearly wants you back. Ernie is still out there. Lock might be captured with Fifi." He sighed. "I'm tempted to lock you up somewhere safe so I know that you're protected, but that didn't work so well the last time."

"We're better together," she said. "Let me fight alongside you."

He considered it and nodded. "I'd be honored. Should we go?"

"Yes," she said. "Let's go quietly, but show me where they were holding Fifi. We'll have to hope we get there before Ernie, if that's where he's going. Then we'll have the element of surprise."

Thor nodded in a direction. "Okay, follow me. This way."

Then he took off on long, strong wolf legs and she went with him, keeping up with every stride. Matched in every way.

For the first time, Matt knew she had truly found her mate. Someone who would let her be their equal, someone who wouldn't leave her behind, and someone who could keep up.

She could hardly wait to get the bad guys so they could go home and seal the deal.

***

Thor tried to calm his pounding heart, the adrenaline pumping through his veins. The urge to kill, the urge to claim, swirled inside him, making it hard to think or breathe.

He hated that she was coming into trouble with him, but she'd be safest by his side. And if he was honest, he'd be safest by hers as well. She made him strong, made him the best wolf he could be, and she was strong too, the perfect mate for him.

But he'd known that for a while. The important thing was that as they ran together, there was a kind of peace between them that made him think she was finally accepting the same thing. That they were made for each other.

They'd been through too much together not to be.

"Thor?" she asked quietly.

"Yes?"

"What is your alpha power?"

"Are you going to be my mate?" he asked. "Because my alpha power isn't very effective once someone knows it, and I tell no one but my family."

"Okay," she said. "If we get out of here okay, I'm going to be your mate. I can't fight it any more."

"Hmph, I was hoping you would come around because I was sexy."

"That too," she said. "But I've always known I needed someone who let me be an equal."

"You're definitely my equal," he said. "You might be even stronger, given what you've been through."

"I doubt that," she said. "And it doesn't need to be one or the other. I'm just glad it's you."

He nodded. "I'm glad it's you."

They galloped on, and he couldn't help laughing at how weird it was. They'd lived such different lives that when they'd first been forced together, they'd hated each other and fought. Now they were making love and fighting by each other's side.

Life could be funny like that sometimes. But still, even with his horrible childhood, the starvation, the fighting, the worries over his brother, looking over at her and knowing that fate had brought her to him, he felt life had been fair with him. More than fair.

He'd go through it all over again for a chance with her.

But he kept his thoughts to himself because they were heading into the forest and needed to be quiet and focused. He heard voices in the distance. Shouting. Pain.

He stopped behind a tree, hidden in the shadows, and Matt bumped into him.

"What?" she asked quietly.

"Shh…"

"You never did tell me your power," she said.

"Shh. They could hear us."

She grumbled something and he kept his ears perked. Someone was wounded, in pain. He darted to a closer tree, and then a closer one, waiting for Matt to follow, and then stopped. The scent in the air had his chest constricting. Someone was dying.

Matt sensed it too. There was no fighting in the clearing right now, so after a nod to Matt, Thor charged forward out of the trees and into the sunlight.

CHAPTER 19

Lock and Fifi were standing next to the SUV, and the man in the suit was on the ground, blood spilling out around him.

"Treacherous…child," he gasped at Fifi, who turned his back on him.

Lock got down on the ground and forced the man to look at him. "You kidnap him, threaten my brother's future mate, and he's the treacherous child?"

"I took you in when you were nothing! Your parents were nothing. Your sister is nothing!"

Fifi snarled but stayed turned away. The man clutched at his suit.

"I'm dying. Damn you, the tribunal will have your head for this. And where is that damned Ernest?"

Thor strode out into the clearing and the man looked up. "You. The twin. Where is the girl?"

Matt walked out behind him, answering his question. "I'm right here. The weak alpha you sent for me wasn't strong enough."

"Damn," the man said. "Should have known."

"Winslow," Matt said, poking the man with her paw as she got close enough. "My father's best friend and second in command."

"Beta?" Thor asked."

"We aren't a pack, so not exactly. More like the doer of dirty work."

"Was," the man said. He was breathing heavily, his chest rising and falling.

"What happened?" she asked Fifi and Lock. Fifi didn't say anything, but Lock faced her.

"He attacked Fifi. I blocked it."

"Attacked? How is Fifi alive?"

"That's the thing," Lock said, folding his arms and coming to stand over the man on the ground. She and Thor stayed in wolf form, looking up at him. "I never guessed he had the ability to kill using his alpha power. See, Thor and I have a unique gift. We can reflect something back if we want to."

"You reflected the attack he made on Fifi?"

"Yup," Lock said. "But I didn't mean to kill him." He knelt down and pressed his finger to the man's neck. Winslow gasped.

"Get away from me."

175

Lock stood. "Suit yourself, but you might change your mind if you knew my other alpha power. See, Lock and I share the reflection. The ability to shield and put someone's attack back on them. But we each have our own power as well. Mine is rapid healing. My blood could save you."

Winslow's eyes widened. They were a dull grayish blue, and the whites of his eyes were tinged red from stress. "Do it."

"I don't know," Lock said. "What are you going to do for me?"

"What do you want?" Winslow asked. His voice was becoming weaker with each word. If they wanted to negotiate, they needed to hurry up.

Personally, Thor wasn't sure he wanted this person saved at all. But if it could be used to get them out of trouble with the tribunal...

"I want you to go back to whomever sent you and tell them to let Matt stay here. Tell them that you can't possibly beat us, and if you try again, we'll make sure the whole wolf world knows what you've done. We have friends in high places, you know. Rowan's family."

Winslow blanched at that, but nodded.

"So tell them that Matt stays here, and they don't so much as try to take her. In return, we stay quiet, and I save your life."

Winslow scowled. "Maybe I should just die so they can come kill you."

Thor growled and took a step forward. This bitter man was their only chance at peace, but it didn't look like a good one. "Maybe you should. And we'll take care of them like they took care of you. Or you can make it easier on all of us by letting us be and telling them to let us be."

He looked at Matt, saw the hope shining in her eyes. Was it really possible? Could they actually be together without fear of the tribunal catching up? Without her pack being threatened?

"Fine," Winslow said. "Do it." He eyed Fifi angrily. "I never thought you'd betray me for the girl. After all I've done."

"All you've done?" Fifi asked drily, stifling a yawn but leaning on the car for strength, still facing away from Winslow. "Funny, but I think that's a reason to indict, rather than praise you."

"You know the rules," he said. "You turn on us…"

"We turn on you. I get it," Fifi said. "You got your chance to kill me. You didn't."

"You need to let Fifi go, too," Lock said.

Fifi shook his head. "I'll go back with them, once I know Matt is safe. That's my world. I never meant to escape it forever. You saved my life, that's enough. Now heal him, and I'll take him back to his miserable family."

"All right," Lock said, holding out a hand to Winslow. "We have witnesses. Pack's promise that you'll do everything you said? And Fifi is safe?"

"Pack's promise," Winslow said. It was the ultimate vow in the wolf world. It couldn't be undone.

It meant a lot to Thor that Lock would do this. Help a man he surely hated and blamed just so that Thor could have the mate he wanted. Lock was finally doing something for the pack. He knelt next to Winslow and took out a knife and Thor looked away, not wanting to watch.

He heard Lock grunt as he cut himself and stayed turned away as Matt came over to join him.

"You think he'll keep his part of the bargain?" she asked.

"I think he has no choice now. And even so, I think the tribunal will think twice about messing with us again."

"Me too," she said.

He nuzzled her as they heard gasping from behind them. Footsteps approached and he turned to see Fifi limping over, coming to kneel by Matt. "I'm glad you're okay. Gosh, I came out here to make sure you were safe and instead I lured everyone into a trap."

"It's okay," she said. "It's all happened so fast, there hasn't been time to think it all out. All that matters to me is that you didn't think, you just came for me. And then you tried to protect my friends and went alone when you thought there was danger. You're truly one of a kind, Fi." She nuzzled his chest.

Thor growled.

"You're one of a kind too," she said. Lock was finishing with Winslow, who was miraculously looking a lot better than a moment ago. Damn, there were some cool mysteries in her world.

"So, you can reflect things?" she asked Thor.

He nodded.

"How come you didn't reflect Fifi?"

He shook his head. "As you saw here, you have to be careful what you are reflecting. If you don't know what power you are sending back on someone, you better use it only on your mortal enemies."

"I guess I should be flattered Lock used it for me then," Fifi said dryly.

Thor laughed. "Well, Lock always was a little more careless than some, but yeah, welcome to the family. If he used the power to protect you, it means you're one of us now." He blinked. "I never in a million years thought I would say that."

"Same to you, Mutt," Fifi said imperiously. "Did you guys bring clothes?"

Thor looked at Matt. "No. So we can't shift yet. We'll just have to wait until they take off."

Winslow stood, brushing his clothes and clearing his throat. After a moment, his face went pale and he staggered to lean with one hand on the side of the black SUV.

"She's more trouble than she's worth anyway," he said. When Thor growled, he put up a hand weakly. "But I'll tell her father she is with a strong alpha who can protect her. That there's no point in pursuing it. And no need, because the secret won't be getting out?" He raised an eyebrow at Matt, who got the point and nodded.

"We can still tell them you married off to some foreigner. And with you up in this remote forest town, no one should know differently. On top of that, who would believe that the son of the tribunal was really a girl?"

A lot of people, given how girly she looked, Thor wanted to say. But he stayed quiet. Everything he wanted was happening all at once. Soon, she would be his forever, with no excuse not to be.

"You have my pack's promise, so you know what that means. Now just don't do anything stupid to draw our attention again." He waved to Fifi. "Fifi, come on."

Fifi bit his lip as Matt nuzzled against him. Thor could tell she didn't want him to go.

"I'll be fine," Fifi said. "His attack wouldn't have killed me. He knows that. He did what he had to do to get to you, but now that you're settled, he has no reason to hurt me."

"Fifi," she said. "There's a life outside of there."

"Not for me," he said. "Not now. Coming, Winslow."

She ducked her head and he could tell she was blinking back tears, but there was no stopping Fifi if he wanted to go. He'd come here without warning and he'd be leaving the same way. "Goodbye," she called.

He said nothing, just raised a hand in a silent wave and then brushed his hair back over his shoulder and got in the SUV.

"What do they have on him?" Thor asked.

"I can't say," she said.

"I'm going to be your mate. Tell me."

"No really, I have a pack's promise with him. I just hope someday he finds someone to tell."

"He will," Lock said, looking over at the car with Fifi in it with that same mysterious expression that he couldn't read. "He's strong." He sighed and shook his head. "And now we're free, and you two should get back to the house. You're trembling."

Thor's eyes widened and he looked at Matt to see his brother was right. She was shaking. "Let's get you back."

"Okay," she said.

"Listen, Fifi's your family. I'm sure he'll come visit. When he's ready to leave that world, he knows you'll be waiting."

"He'll never be ready," she said. "But you're right. He'd want me to be happy." She stood on shaky legs. "Race you back to the house?"

Thor grinned. "Sure."

Lock rubbed the back of his neck. "Um, I'm going to just go clean up at the local bed and breakfast. I'm guessing you two are going to need some alone time."

"Damn straight we are," Thor said, and Matt laughed. The sound warmed him from the toes up. Lock transformed and took off in the direction of the town, and Thor rubbed his shoulder against his mate. "Come on, Mate. Let's go home."

CHAPTER 20

When they were back at the house, Matt felt an odd sense of relief, but also a lot of pain and sadness. On the one hand, she was glad to be back with Thor, and now they had no reason they couldn't mate.

On the other, Fifi was back with the tribunal. All she could hope was that someday he'd have an opportunity to escape, that someday someone could rescue him the way he'd rescued her.

She collapsed after shifting and let Thor carry her into his bedroom and set her on the bed. He walked into the bathroom and turned on the water.

"I thought you might like a bath," he said.

She sighed. What she wanted was to be mated to him, but her body just wasn't cooperating. The effects of the drug were lingering, and she felt weak and tired. Exhausted physically and emotionally. All she wanted was to wash the day away, wash Ernie's touch away...

She jerked her head up. "Wait, Ernie..."

"You saw him run," Thor said. "He won't be back. He knows I can kick his ass. He knows even a female can kick his ass if he doesn't have those darts. Nevertheless, I'm going to nail the front door shut while you take your bath."

She coughed. "Nail it shut?"

He nodded, looking pleased with himself. "To make sure he doesn't try anything with the key he has. I gave it to him in case of emergency. I swear, if I'd ever thought he would betray me…"

"I know," she said. "Despite what's happened to you, you want to trust people. There's nothing wrong with that. And you saved me before anything could happen. So I'm fine."

"Good," he said. "The bathroom's in there. I'mma go nail the front door shut."

She laughed drily, but felt herself heat up as she watched him go, his large back and shoulders seeming so wide and strong. So hers. She giggled and grabbed a towel from the chair and went into the bathroom.

A few minutes later she was warm and dry, wearing a terry cloth robe that had been hanging in the shower, and walking into the living room to see Thor kneeling adorably in front of the door, a couple of nails held between his lips as he hammered away.

"I think you've probably got it covered."

"No one is going to bother my mate," he mumbled around the nails.

"And how are we going to get out of here?" she asked.

He sighed. He was wearing a tee shirt that showed off his impressive muscles, and his dark hair was tousled, damp from sweat and exertion. "I'm not worried about that. Not until we find Ernie. But first, we need some privacy." He grinned at her.

"Oh, do we?" she asked, playing with the belt of her robe, letting it fall open a little to give him a glimpse of slim leg.

Nails clattered to the floor as his jaw dropped, and he stood quickly leaving the door behind and coming to sweep her up into his arms.

"Woah, Cowboy," she said.

"Call me whatever you want," he said. "As long as you are ready to call me mate."

"I am," she said, snuggling in against his chest. She didn't even care that he was a little sweaty. She just wanted to make love to him. To feel him all over her, owning her, right now. And she wanted to know that he was hers as well.

"You want me to shower?" he asked, kicking open the door to her bedroom.

"No," she said, raising an eyebrow as he dropped her on the bed. "You want to go into the master?"

He shook his head. "No. This is where I first kissed you. This is where I first wanted to claim you. Where my wolf was howling to take you. This is where I'm finally going to give him what he wants."

"Is it what you want?" she asked.

"Are you kidding? I am him. He's me. We both get you, we both want you."

"That's even more confusing," she said, giggling.

His face warmed. "I love your laugh." He reached out a finger to softly stroke her jaw. "I want to hear that as much as possible from now on."

She smirked. "That shouldn't be a problem. You make me laugh all the time. Even when you don't want to."

"This is true," he said. "But there is never a time I don't want you to."

"When I look at your penis?"

He frowned. "Okay, maybe not then. But come on, who is going to laugh at that?" He gave her a smirk and she rolled her eyes.

"You're right. It's far too scary. Too intimidating, too—mph."

He cut off her words with an intense, tender kiss. One that seemed to go on and on with only the sound of her heartbeat to keep time. After a moment, she wrapped her arms up and around him, circling his back and neck, and he sighed against her lips and deepened the kiss, swiping wetly against her tongue.

She moaned. Everything he did felt amazing, and she knew it wasn't simply because she'd gone without for so long. There was something running underneath it all, beneath the pleasure and the sensuality. There was a love there, and she thought that that must be what fated mates meant. And she liked it.

He pulled at the belt of her robe and she helped him untie it. Then he knelt between her spread legs and pulled the robe open, baring her to him.

"You're so beautiful," he said. "So fucking beautiful that I can't possibly deserve you."

"That's not true," she said. "I'm a pain in the ass. Stubborn, willful…"

"Well, I'm a pain in the ass too," he said. "I need you to keep me in line."

"I can do that," she said, burying one hand in his hair as his lips found her breast. "Oh gosh, Thor. Don't stop."

He sent her a wicked grin and swirled his tongue around her nipple, using a hand to gently tweak her other breast that was longing for his attention. When both were standing in stiff peaks, he switched, taking the other in his mouth and soothing the wet one with his hand. It was so gentle, so attentive, and it made her body come alive in places she hadn't known existed. She felt on fire. When he was done torturing her breasts with delicious swipes of his tongue he grinned and moved down her body.

He licked wickedly over her navel and she arched, and then he parted her legs even farther and kept his strong hands on her thighs as he leaned down to kiss her right at her center. She squirmed, but his hands on her legs kept her helpless to the onslaught of pleasure, so all she could do was bite her lip and twist her hands into the covers as he stroked and kissed her toward a tidal wave of sensation.

When it came, refreshing and intense and wonderful now that she knew they were safe, she arched up and he caught her in his arms. She kissed him as she came, tasting herself on him, loving the way his hands gripped her, letting her know she was safe to feel all of this with him.

When her muscles were calming, he let her fall back against the pillow and started again.

"You're torturing me," she gasped out, watching him lock eyes with her as he swirled his tongue against her most intimate area. "I can't take it."

"Oh, you can take it. And you love it," he said, flicking his tongue over her. She closed her eyes and put her head back. Damn it, he was right. She loved it and he better not stop.

"Tell me you love it," he said.

"I love it," she grated out. "But you know that."

"I do," he said, setting a hand on her stomach to calm her, making her feel sexy as he felt along her smooth skin. "I love how you let me know it with your incredible body. I love the sounds you make and the scent in the air." He kissed her gently, slowing things down slightly. He sat up on his knees and reached a hand down to touch her. "More than anything, I just love you," he said. Then his finger circled and then pressed down right over her and another orgasm hit, even harder than before.

He loved her. She opened her eyes to focus on his handsome face, those glowing sunset eyes, that strong jaw, flexing slightly as he kept his eyes on her, drinking in every second of her pleasure. It was so hot how he understood her. How he treated her like she was the only person who existed at this moment.

And now she couldn't wait to see him go through the same thing. To see his eyes tighten with pleasure so strong it was almost unbearable, and know that she was the one who had given it to him.

He reached for her and held her tight, and her heart pounded in rhythm with his. "Marry me. Mate me. Always stay with me."

"Always," she said, holding him back. "Thor?"

"Yes?"

"I'm ready." She lay back against the bed, spreading her legs for him in invitation as she shrugged out of the robe. A muscle in his jaw twitched. He didn't need to be told twice. He pulled off his shirt and hopped out of the jeans he'd hastily thrown on when they got back.

He stood before her naked. Her alpha.

He knelt in front of her. "Ready?"

"I've never been more ready for anything in my life," she said.

He grinned and reached for her, testing her wetness. Then he put his finger up to his mouth and slowly licked it off, keeping eye contact with her as he did. That was embarrassing as hell, but a little hot. No, a lot hot.

"Damn you, get inside me right now," she said.

"As you wish, princess," he said, lifting her thighs to wrap her legs around him. She locked her heels and felt him at her entrance. So she locked her legs tighter and lifted her hips, taking him slowly inside her as he let out a hoarse gasp.

"Damn it, let a man get adjusted," he gasped out. "You're too much, princess."

"I'm not a princess anymore," she said. "I'm your queen."

"My queen," he said. "Have mercy on your subject. I'm not going to last long with you gripping me like that."

She grinned. "Then hurry up."

He grumbled something but grinned at her as she loosened her legs slightly so he could stroke out and then in. She lit up inside as each inch of his length stimulated her most sensitive areas. Damn, he felt good. So huge, filling her completely. He was impossible to ignore, and she loved it. She loved the way his face tensed each time he was fully sheathed inside her, loved the focus in his eyes as he tried to stay grounded so he could please her. Loved the rising pressure building within her.

She knew when it exploded, it would be magical, unlike anything she had known. Because as the pleasure within her rose, so did an awareness of something greater than her. A connection with him and the universe, and their wolves. It reminded her of starry nights watching the sky, of meteor showers, of anything that makes you feel a part of something so much bigger than you are.

And then as he withdrew once more and then sheathed himself inside her, she felt her pleasure hit a peak and then explode into light, and clutched onto him as she felt him jerk in response, spilling his seed inside her. She felt his release from within, pulsing against her. Felt his breath, hot and warm as he murmured words of love and promises of forever.

Felt her wolf running free though the forest with a dark red wolf beside her.

"I love you," she gasped in his ear as she rode out the last of her orgasm. "I'll always love you."

"Good," he said, taking her mouth in a harsh kiss. "Because I'm yours."

Gosh, that felt good to hear. And it was true. He raised up on his hands and let out a low howl into the night, letting everyone know how he felt claiming his mate.

She wanted to howl with him, but could only hold him, the words reverberating in her mind. I'm yours. I'm yours.

"I'm yours," she said back.

"Forever," he said. "My whole lifetime."

"Longer," she said.

"If it's possible." He collapsed against her, warm body resting atop hers. She loved the pleasant weight of him, the feel of his muscles. "I want it to be."

She stroked his hair. "Me too."

He pulled out and held her against his chest in the dark. All she could hear was their breathing, their heart beats.

When she'd left her family a week ago, she'd never thought she'd be here now, with the perfect mate, the perfect defender.

But fate worked in mysterious ways, and now the red thread that had led her to Thor had bonded them together forever. She couldn't think of a single thing she needed.

She was happy.

Thor fell asleep first, his arm heavy around her, keeping her safe and letting her know he was there. And she found herself going over all of their moments together, treasuring each one.

And then, as she grew sleepy and fought to stay awake so that the moment wouldn't end, she realized that the next day could be just as wonderful as this one, and the next and the next after that could as well. Because Thor would be there to see to it.

She kissed his brow and fell asleep in his arms.

She was finally free.

EPILOGUE

"Are you sure you won't stay?" Thor asked, fiddling with the glass in front of him on the table. Matt sat next to him, poking at the eggs he'd fixed her. All attempts to fatten his mate up in the last few weeks had failed, but he hadn't given up hope.

And as long as she felt happy and cared for, what else mattered?

"I'm sure," Lock said. "There's nothing left for me here. You're alpha and you're doing a great job."

"Thanks," Thor said. "But you know you're welcome."

Lock stretched and the dark brown leather of his jacket crinkled. "I still have things to do."

Matt flicked her gaze to him. "You aren't going to go after the tribunal, are you?"

"No," Lock said. But his eye twitched slightly, and Thor would bet he was lying.

"Don't mess with it," Thor said, shaking his head. "Stay here. Find someone to settle down with. You know, Lily asked about you the other day. Come to think of it, she never stopped asking about you."

Lock sighed. "No. You know that wouldn't work. And I'm really not going after the tribunal, at least not what you might think. The last thing I want is to cause trouble for you and Lacey. But I have a debt to repay."

"I think we should keep calling her Matt. She answers to it more readily."

"Don't talk about me like I'm not here," Matt grumbled. "But yes, for better or worse, that's my name."

Thor grinned and put an arm around her, pulling her close so he could place a kiss on her head. He loved being able to do that whenever he wanted to. Being able to do lots of things whenever we wanted to. He licked his lips.

"Save it for the bedroom," Lock said. "Or at least after I'm gone."

"We're newly mated," Thor said. "We can't help it."

"We don't want to help it," Matt said, grinning back at him.

"Gross," Lock said, standing to leave. "Well, then, I'm off."

"At least give me an idea of where you're going."

Lock tilted his head, sending his longish, dark red hair off to the side. "I can tell you I'm going to go visit another pack. Some friends of ours."

"Oh no, Rowan's family?"

Lock nodded. "They deserve to know about Misty's family. And they're smart. They won't engage the tribunal lightly."

"That's kind of smart in a way," Matt said. "Then it's not you getting involved."

"I just think they should know," Lock said. But Thor didn't fully believe him. As long as he kept the trouble away from his mate and his pack though, he'd be fine with it.

"Be careful," Thor said. "If you get in trouble, we won't be there to bail you out this time."

"Hey, this time I bailed you out, so I think we're even. And I won't get in trouble. My business after visiting Rowan's pack has nothing to do with you. Don't worry about me."

"Impossible," Thor said, standing to give his brother a hearty hug while his mate watched. "Tell us when you get where you're going safely. At least keep us informed."

"I'll do my best," Lock said. Then he waved to Matt, and let himself out the front door. Thor watched him go and then slowly shut the door.

He couldn't help feeling a little down, a little worried, but his brother was his own man. And he had others to worry about. Particularly his mate, who was clearly done with her meal and was looking at him like she was hungry for something more satisfying.

He grinned. "The bedroom?"

She nodded. "Yup."

He laughed and swooped her up in his arms. He loved everything about her. Her short hair, her way of trying to act or sound like a boy at certain moments, the way she was already trying to worry about his pack.

He'd say he'd chosen the right mate, but really, she'd chosen him. Walked right to him on a night where he was staying up with the moonlight. Came in soaking wet and proceeded to turn his life upside down.

He set her on his bed, but instead of joining her immediately, pulling something out of his bedstead table. He'd had it polished this morning and sized, and couldn't wait to see her reaction when he gave it to her.

He sat on the bed nervously, and she cocked her head to the side and gave him a grin.

"What's wrong, babe?"

He held out the box. "Here."

"You look nervous," she said. "You never look nervous."

"That's because I'm not afraid of anyone," he said. "But now that I have you, I'm a little afraid of messing up."

She laughed. "As you should be," she joked, trying to figure out how to open the antique box. "What is it?"

She was wearing sweats and a hoodie, as usual. She still liked comfortable, boyish clothes, and it was so her that he loved them to. He pretty much loved everything she did, and got more and more sickeningly into her every day.

"Here, let me help," he said, taking it from her and undoing the little latch. He handed it back.

A ring sparkled up at her. It had an antique diamond in the center, surrounded by a tiny halo of small antique diamonds that glittered together like a ball of fire. "It's been in the family for many years. I know you're not into human things, and you aren't really into jewelry, but I wanted you to have it. So that those who do follow human norms know who you belong to."

She just stared at it for a second, brushing her hand behind one ear. Then she looked up at him and threw her arms around her neck. "It's perfect." She slid it on her finger. "It fits perfectly."

"Of course, I had it sized."

"How did you know my size? I don't wear any rings."

He grinned, baring a fang. "I bought a sizer and measured you when you were asleep."

"Vaguely creepy," she said. "But it's a perfect fit."

"Thanks, I'm glad. You know what else is a perfect fit?" he said, intertwining his hands with hers and pressing her back against the bedspread.

She laughed. "I think I know where you're going with this."

He nuzzled in against her neck and she gasped and then sighed as he kissed a line up to her ear. He kissed her lobe gently, teasing it with his tongue.

"I like my ring on you," he said.

"Thor?" she asked. "There's still one thing bothering me. What's your alpha power?"

"Reflecting?" he asked.

"No, the one you don't share with Lock."

"Oh, I can immobilize shifters."

She shivered slightly. "Wow, dangerous."

"Only if someone messed with me," he said. "Or you. Definitely if anyone came near you and I didn't want them to."

"So you can immobilize people, hm?" she asked, running a hand up his arm. Damn, it felt good when she touched him. He nodded, throat tight.

"Maybe you should show me this power," she said, running her hands up his chest and driving him crazy.

He loved tying her up sometimes, watching her writhe under more pleasure than she could take. But he wasn't going to use something that was a weapon on her, no matter how harmless it could be.

"I don't need an alpha power to make love to you sweetheart. But I promise that if anyone ever threatened you, you'd see all of my power and then some."

She flushed and continued to stroke his arm. "I see. I just kind of want to see how it works."

He nipped at her ear and she sighed. "I think I can make it up to you."

"You're welcome to try," she gasped out as he licked the edge of her ear. She was extra sensitive there.

"Try? I don't try. I do. And the only alpha power that matters is the power I have to be your alpha and yours alone. The only one who can make you feel like I do."

"Prove it," she said breathlessly.

So he did.

ABOUT THE AUTHOR

Terry Bolrdyer loves writing sexy paranormal romance and reading sexy paranormal romance. You can reach her at terrybolryder.com or by email at terrybolryder@yahoo.com.

Thanks for reading!

10059536R00118

Printed in Great Britain
by Amazon.co.uk, Ltd.,
Marston Gate.